CURTIS HARRELL

Melpomene's Garden

First published by Sley House Publishing LLC 2022

"Melpomene's Garden" first appeared in Tales of Sley House 2021.

"Liar" was first published at www.fleasonthedog.com.

The Corner of Victory and Van Nuys first appeared in The Cave Region Review.

"The Tehachapi Sheriff Buries His Native Wife Circa 1900" first appeared in Eclectica.

"After Harvest" first appeared in Descant.

"Freeing the Sparrow" first appeared in College of the Canyon's Poets and Writers.

"Pride and Joy" first appeared in The Old Time News, Friends of American Old Time Music and Dance.

"The Last Thing You Wanted" first appeared in The Healing Muse.

"Ice Storm" first appeared in The Healing Muse.

"Insurance Trilogy" first appeared in riprap journal as well as being reprinted in The Low Valley Review.

"Whippoorwill" first appeared in The Cave Region Review.

"History" first appeared in The Cave Region Review.

"Equinox" first appeared in The Cave Region Review.

"The Last Tattoo Poem" first appeared in The Tattooed Poets Blog.

"Fossil" first appeared in Allegro Poetry Magazine.

First edition

ISBN: 978-1-7373102-4-2

This book was professionally typeset on Reedsy.
Find out more at reedsy.com

This book is dedicated to my wife, Vicki, my daughters, Autumn and Summer, my parents, Curtis Sr. and Marva, and my mentors, Truen, Claude, Jim, and the Escribos.

Contents

Preface

Stories

I was very fortunate that my parents were believers in books and reading. I remember the thrill and anticipation I felt when my teacher handed out the Weekly Reader Book Club order forms when I was in elementary school. I looked forward to getting home after school and poring over the titles, the enticing little pictures of the book covers. From the beginning I had a fascination with the mysterious. Even though I was occasionally tempted by books about baseball, my first choices were always the collections of ghost stories or monster tales or unexplained phenomena. And my parents' support and encouragement allowed me to buy these books that took me into a shadowy world, a world with the macabre around every corner. In fact, now, 50 years later, I still have most, if not all, of those books in my basement library. In my family, books were sacred objects, never to be discarded.

I don't know exactly why I was drawn to the supernatural. Perhaps it was because I remembered listening to my dad's stories as we traveled in the car to my grandparents' house. It was a drive that took a little under an hour, but, about halfway there, we went through a small town in western Tennessee where a huge cotton mill stood. My dad traveled around the county in his job as an insurance claims adjuster, and that's probably where he heard some of the stories he told. The cotton mill had several huge warehouses, and my dad told the stories of the things the nightwatchmen encountered as they patrolled the cavernous buildings in the wee, black hours after midnight as they made their rounds. Sometimes, late on Sunday evenings as we returned home, we would pass the warehouses, illuminated by mercury vapor lights, and I would imagine a lone watchman peering into the darkness with his flashlight.

Another story warned of ghostly presences in abandoned houses, one in particular that was also on the way to my grandparents' house. An abandoned house sat back from the two lane asphalt road at an angle. The roof sagged in a few places, but the windows were all intact. As we approached, a light would appear in a window, and, as we passed, the light would move from room to room as if something were following us as we intruded past the derelict shell. I was too young to realize that the light was our own headlights, and I preferred the ominous possibility that a former inhabitant still wandered the empty rooms.

As I grew, I kept a wary eye out for things that pushed the boundaries of what could be explained away. When I was in 5th grade our family moved to an old house in Cleveland, Ohio. In addition to being unfamiliar, it was also just plain creepy. I recall that on the first night we stayed there after the movers had unloaded all of our furniture and belongings, we, my mom, dad, sister, and I, sat at the kitchen table when we heard a rhythmic creak emanating from the living room. I distinctly remember the hesitation every one of us felt before we slowly walked to the door to peer into the darkened living room. There, in the middle of the room on the hardwood floor, our rocking chair moved back and forth by itself. Months later, as my mom folded laundry in the basement, she heard someone walking in the room above her, and, when she rushed upstairs, she found no one in the room and the house securely locked.

What cemented my preoccupation with otherworldly occurrences happened when I was in grad school at the University of Arkansas. I shared a huge old house with two brothers, friends of mine. It sat just off the Fayetteville square, facing South College Avenue with Archibald Yell Boulevard looming over the backyard. The very first night I spent in that house, I woke abruptly from a deep sleep to see a man standing in my bedroom doorway. He was short, with dark hair and cropped dark beard, and he was smoking a cigarette. I could see the cherry brighten as he took a drag and dim as he exhaled. Strangely, I was not so much afraid as I was curious, and then slightly angered at the idea of an intruder. I reached for my glasses, and, when I looked back at the door, he was gone. I jumped up and searched the house, but my roommates were sound asleep, the house was otherwise empty, and all of the doors and windows were locked. I shrugged it off despite feeling certain my sighting of the man had really happened.

The next day, a few of the people who had previously lived in the house came by to get some of their belongings out of a shed in the backyard. As we sat and visited after they had loaded their pickup, talk somehow came around to certain events, or happenings, that had occurred in the house. The pit of my stomach fell when they asked who had the last room on the left in the upper hallway. That was my room. I guess my expression changed as I told them, and the young man asked if I had already seen him. I described the short, dark man, and they immediately confirmed that was the nocturnal visitor who appeared on occasion.

Later that year, I returned from a school trip to an empty house, my roommates having gone home for Thanksgiving. As I fumbled with my keys at the front door, the phone began ringing. Despite the amount of time it took me to open the door, the ringing persisted, and, as I rushed to answer the phone, I tumbled headlong over an overstuffed chair that had been dragged out to the middle of room. I scrambled to the ringing phone, but, as soon as I answered, the line went dead. Cursing my roommates for rearranging the furniture in my absence I walked to bottom of the staircase and flipped on the light. There, at the top of the stairs, was the dark man, and he glanced down at me before he ducked into the huge room that was over the living room. Again, not so much afraid as curious and angered, I rushed up the staircase into the pitch-black room. I flicked on the light to find it empty. There was a walk-in closet at one end, the door closed. I slowly turned the knob and swung open the door. I had to take four steps into the room to pull the string on the ceiling light, and, after I had yanked it on, I discovered the closet empty as well. There was an old armoire, large enough to conceal a person, against the wall, and I grabbed the handle and pulled it open. The armoire was empty as well. When I related this story to my roommates, they revealed that neither of them had moved any furniture.

But the event that sealed my appreciation for the possibility of forces working and existing outside of our known realm happened a few days after that. I was sitting in the living room, reading, when I heard a banging sound coming from an empty bedroom off of the dining room, the door to that room clearly visible from the couch where I sat. I rose and opened the door to find nothing out of the ordinary. It was mid-afternoon, the sky overcast with a cold November gloom. I closed the door and returned to my reading only to hear the banging noises repeated. Once again I scanned the empty room and saw nothing unusual. But, when I returned to my book, the banging resumed. Half-jokingly I said out loud, "If you're a ghost, give me a true sign instead of this banging crap." Suddenly the banging tripled in intensity. I ran to the bedroom door and flung it open. Immediately inside the door, to the right, was the back of a metal heater that warmed the bathroom on the other side of the wall. The bottom of the metal was louvered, a vent for the heater, and I noticed, for the first time, a piece pf paper barely protruding through the vent. Startled that a potential fire hazard existed, I grabbed a screwdriver from the trunk of my car and removed the vent. When I did, a stack of about a dozen magazines slid onto the floor. They were old Look magazines. Joking again, I said to the empty room, "So is this your big sign?" But I felt my spine go cold when I noticed that the date on the top magazine, the one I held in my hand, was dated October 13th, 1958. My exact birthday.

So I guess you could say that I come to my preoccupation with the spirit world honestly. In the years after grad school I met a lovely woman and married, and we had two daughters. I was teaching at an experimental high school for at-risk students, and beside the satisfaction I found working with these brilliant kids, I had summers off. I took advantage one summer when my daughters were little to write some stories that depended on elements of the supernatural. I drew on my memories of all of the books I had bought when I was their age. I also drew on more traditional literary traditions, like the Southern Gothic tales of William Faulkner. For me, "A Rose for Emily" was the perfect story with its shocking ending. So I modeled my stories after these influences.

Not all of the stories have a ghost per se, but they all have hints of ghosts, or things that are surprising and unexpected. An emphasis is on the twisty plot in this collection as well as the fun involved in keeping an open mind. I had originally intended my audience to be young adults, but I discovered that the appeal of the fiction transcended any age group, even though many of my protagonists are school age.

"The Woman Who Was Afraid of Dying" was inspired by my experiences with Latino students and the cultures I found in southern California. I wrote "The Scent of Baby Powder" to deal with the death of my stillborn son. My grandfather originally told me the story that is the conclusion of "The Rattler's Tale." "A Simple Act of Kindness" recalls my actual experiences as a crossing guard in grade school although nothing supernatural occurred on my watch, thank goodness. I am sort of miffed about "The Insomniac" because I wrote this story many years before the movie *The Sixth Sense*. "Daffodils" is perhaps the least supernatural tale in the collection, but it incorporates many details from my life and my love of my grandfather. I wrote "One Last Battle" as a tribute to my family members who had served in WWII. "Melpomene's Garden" was fun to write because I incorporated a poem into the story. The words spoken by the young lady character are in iambic pentameter. "The Killer Tattoo" is close to my heart because I am myself heavily tattooed, so I have experience in a tattoo parlor. "Liar" is the only story written recently, and I think you'll find the tone and language a bit different and more mature, but I think it still fits right in with the collection.

I hope each reader finds something enjoyable in the stories. I think that, overall, the tone of the ghost stories I loved as a child permeate these narratives. I also hope that the themes are instructive, as well, now in a world where the strange is not always rare or unexpected. Hopefully ghosts can, in addition to scaring us, redeem us as well.

Plays

The community college where I taught for many years had a theatre department that usually put on a production once a semester. I have enjoyed acting in amateur plays since I was in high school, and I became the go-to guy if a part required a long beard! As a result I have performed as Gloucester in *King Lear*, the good duke in *As You Like It*, a town elder in *The Crucible*, a museum guard in *The Shape of Things*, and the title role in *The Giver*, among many other roles. Sitting through so many rehearsals really piqued my curiosity about how plays are written, so I wrote a couple.

The Corner of Victory and Van Nuys recalls a tattoo parlor I visited fairly often back in the 1980s. I got interested in the idea of body art but also the vagabond character. In these plays I became more concerned with character development than plot. In some ways, the plays, though plotted like a story, were more like writing poetry since each of the lines was very important. So I focused on giving each of the characters something interesting to say.

Duke Sims and the Duchess of Russia was fun to write because I really did live in Cleveland, Ohio in the summer of 1969. It was quite a momentous year, and I reference a few of the events that made that summer famous. What was the most fun was that I discovered a website that lists all of the box scores for virtually all major league baseball games going back to the fifties or earlier. So, when I have Vincent tell Mrs. Novak a score or have him describe some play, the details are taken directly from authentic box scores. All of the baseball details really happened as Vincent describes them.

Poems

My primary training as a writer is in writing poetry. I received an MFA in Creative Writing with an emphasis on contemporary British and American poetry from the University of Arkansas. As I compiled the poems for this collection, it dawned on me how eclectic my poetic style is. I've written sonnets and free verse, long poems and short. So, in some ways the poems fit in to the volume better, I think, because of the generally eclectic compilation of three different genres.

I do have to admit that there were two classes I took in grad school that made me think like a writer. The first, oddly enough, was Claude Faulkner's Composition for Teachers course. We grad assistants had to take that course to prepare ourselves to teach, and the course really finally forced me to thoroughly grasp and understand grammar. Although I was a natural writer because of all the reading I had done since childhood, a few major usage errors would still pop up in my writing. After taking the grammar course, I had a facility and an instinctual insight into how language worked. I compare it to the moment a musician finally masters an instrument and making each note becomes effortless.

The other course was Poetic Form and Theory taught by Jim Whitehead. In that class I received a masterful grounding in the traditional forms of poetry as well as the reasons and skills needed for creating free verse. Jim deeply loved several poems, and he taught to love them too.

The Stories

The Woman Who Was Afraid of Dying

It all began with the ghost of a bird. Cesar first saw it the night of his grandfather's funeral, as he sat in the living room of his grandfather's house. Even this small room, crowded with mementos and knickknacks and hundreds of framed photographs, seemed empty as he listened to his grandmother mutter and sob from her well-worn easy chair. As Cesar stood beside her chair and tried to make things better by rubbing the back of her age-speckled hand clenching the arm of the faded recliner, he saw the shadow darting back and forth in the corner of the room. At first he thought that the shadow belonged to a moth circling the bulb beneath the red, tasseled shade of the only lamp in the room. But, as he strained his eyes to peer past the glare and tried to listen for the frantic tell-tale tapping of the moth against the paper shade, he became aware of what his grandmother mumbled between the sharp intakes of breath as she stifled her crying.

"Why did you leave me, Papa?" she whispered to herself, "why did you leave me here all by myself?"

"Rest easy, Old Meja," Cesar murmured as he stroked her hand.

"Rest easy?" the old woman croaked, suddenly wild-eyed as she yanked her hand from Cesar's grasp, "I cannot rest easy. Your grandpapa and I have been together for fifty-two years. Since I was a young girl, hardly older than you, your grandpapa has been with me. The very first time we met, he promised me that he would never leave me, that he would be with me always."

"And now," she whispered, "I am all alone."

"But Old Meja," Cesar said, his voice small and choked, "he didn't mean to leave you now. He couldn't help it. You will see him again one day."

"No," she wailed, slumping to her knees "no, no, no. You cannot understand. It is me who has broken the promise. It is me who is selfish and afraid."

"Old Meja, please…"

"No, you are right. I should see Papa again one day, but I am so afraid. If I were given the choice to see him again at my death or to live forever so I would never have to endure my spirit escaping in my last breath, I would choose to walk the earth until the end of time."

The stillness of the room, at that second, burst with the cacophony of frenzied wings, and so many shadows darted around the ceiling it was if a horde of bats had been loosed in the tiny room. The old photographs, sepia-toned with age, lurched and quivered in the shimmer of the racing shadows. Cesar and his grandmother cowered on the floor, their heads covered with their arms.

"Heaven help us," Cesar's grandmother moaned and flailed the air.

Then there was silence, except for the infinitesimal scratching of sparrow claws on polished oak. But it was not a sparrow. There, on the carved frame of her wedding picture, twitched the apparition of a mockingbird. No longer merely a flitting shadow, the mockingbird had taken form and color, its back dark gray and its belly pale. The black bars on its wings became nearly solid, but the specter was transparent, the way the stained-glass image of a bird on a lamp shade is translucent when the bulb is burning.

"The eye, Cesar," Old Meja whimpered, "can you see the eye?"

Cesar looked at the eye, and he could not answer. The coal-black bead of the mockingbird's eye shone and flickered as if it concealed the conflagration of its very soul. As Cesar stammered to respond, the mockingbird opened its beak to call, and the sound that echoed through the room was not the sweet warble of the thrasher or the red song of the cardinal but a raven's croak. That throaty screak made the walls tremble, and the mockingbird then wheeled on its strange perch and glared at the old woman cringing on the floor.

"Cesar," gasped his grandmother, "I have seen this bird before, a long time ago, when I was young."

The mockingbird caracoled to the back of the easy chair and curiously cocked his bright eye toward her.

"When we were first married, Papa and I worked the farms up north. At the beginning of our third season together, Louis, Papa's little brother, was to be married to Maria, my little sister."

Cesar's gaze, from memory, went to the photograph hanging beneath his grandparent's wedding picture. The image was faded from the decades it had spent hanging in the same spot on the newspapered wall, but it still clearly showed a gangly young man in a stiff dress coat gently holding to him a small, dark woman gazing fondly at something outside the boundaries of the photograph. A tiny ivory cameo necklace hung from the frame. This was their engagement picture, posed before the cavernous mouth of a dilapidated barn. Cesar knew this was the only picture of the couple, and he was startled when the mockingbird, with a devilish pirouette, landed on its frame and made the pendant tremble.

"There was more rain that spring than even the oldest men could remember," his grandmother continued, her voice distant, her eyes glazed, "and we were worried because the fields we were working were bottom land near the Kings River. Louis and Maria were to be married on a Sunday morning, and we had planted in the rain all day on Saturday so the bosses wouldn't complain about our taking the next afternoon for the wedding party. It was still raining Sunday morning as we gathered inside the seed barn for the priest to marry them. I was Maria's bridesmaid, and she had fussed at me all morning about keeping her bridal train from getting muddy. They were husband and wife for less than half a day."

Old Meja paused, and her vacant eyes welled with tears. The mockingbird impatiently whirled and scrabbled from his perch. The room filled with the humid scent of rain.

"I had just finished serving the cake, and we were standing at the door of the barn, watching the rain, when we saw the strangest sight. From the trees by the creek, wild animals fled in every direction into the muddy fields. Three deer raced right through the barn, nearly touching us as they passed. Then we heard a roar over the rustle and splash of the coyotes and rabbits and deer rushing from the tall grass into the fields, and we saw the big trees bend double and fall. One bear came scrambling out of the brush, and, no sooner than we saw him, the water rolled up behind him and lifted him up like a toy, and I heard him bawl until he went under.

"Papa grabbed my hand and pulled me through the barn, but I fell. And instead of following him, I foolishly ran to the ladder to the loft where Papa and I slept. I climbed into the straw and snatched my velvet jewelry bag from the box at the head of our blankets. Then, when I stumbled back to the ladder, the barn, the whole world, spun around and came loose."

Cesar, though transfixed by his grandmother's rasping monologue, became aware, through the periphery of his sight, of the gathering of shadows again in the corners of the ceiling. Faintly, they flocked with the barely audible rush of flowing water.

"Everything was floating. The loft had come apart, and I clung to an empty cider keg. The water was dark and full of brush. Everything was grasping at my legs beneath the water. Snakes swirled by wrapped around limbs of fallen trees. A washtub bobbed up and banged my head. A rope with laundry still pinned to it wrapped around my barrel then caught in the top of a tree and spun me around like a top. Finally I was snared in the branches of a huge oak. The current pressed me against the trunk and raged in a torrent over my back and head. I climbed until I was out of the water. My legs were bleeding, and I had lost my best shoes.

"It was then that I saw the mockingbird. He was perched above me in the tree, and he had gone mad. He croaked and cawed as he skittered from one branch to another. He hung upside down and snatched at my hair. He was trying to drive me from the tree, as if he had forgotten that he could fly to safety and was afraid that my weight would tumble his sanctuary from the flood. His incessant caterwauling petrified me, and I closed my eyes and hugged the tree with all of my strength.

"As I perilously clung above the rushing water, I heard voices through the mockingbird's din. The voices were desperate and calling my name. I tremulously shifted my position on the tree and saw, over my shoulder, that the turmoil of the deluge had washed Maria and Louis into the limbs of a tree nearly within reach of me. A rope was tied to their refuge and stretched taut above the water to the bank where Papa had secured the other end to another tree. They were so close. Maria straddled a branch and inched her way toward me, her arm outstretched. The freshet had stripped her of her wedding train and dress, and she crawled toward me in her muddy petticoat. I tried to loosen my grasp on the trunk and reach for her hand, but the mockingbird pitched and swooped at my tenuous grip on the rough bark. I could hear Maria pleading with me to try to reach her. I could see her eyes, frightened and determined, the same expression she wore when we were children and Louis dared her to jump into the pond from the highest branch of the pine tree. She inched even closer and shouted at me to reach for her hand. I never loved her more than I did at that second, but I was too afraid to let go of the trunk. I was too afraid of the muddy, roiling water. I was too afraid of that sinister bird. As I clung selfishly to that cold haven, Maria crept ever further out toward me, and the branch she cleaved to, under her weight, dipped into the turbid rush, and she was ripped away. Louis lunged for her hand, but he too was swallowed by the deluge. Fishermen found them a week later, embracing one another beneath a sunken log."

Cesar's gasp made his grandmother abruptly stir from the daze of her memory. The shadows swarmed the walls of the room hysterically. Cesar and his grandmother seemed to be in the eye of a storm of hellish moths, and their dappled rush caused the parlor to spin sickeningly. Then, from out of the rim of the cyclone into the still eddy where Cesar and his grandmother helplessly waited, wafted the diaphanous forms of Maria and Louis. Old Meja threw herself before the stern-faced apparitions and wailed. The mockingbird cackled and crazily gyrated around Old Meja's prostrated figure.

"Please leave me," Old Meja keened, "please leave me alone. Seek no vengeance on this old fool. I have suffered enough. I have suffered every day of my life for my part in your tragedy. Please leave me."

But the wraiths glided even closer to Old Meja, until they hovered directly before the place where she cowered. Cesar clearly recognized the couple because they appeared exactly as they did in the old photograph. Louis wore the same stiff coat, and Maria still nestled in his clasp, but now she no longer gazed abstractedly away into the distance. She glared down at Old Meja with the same dour expression that cloaked Louis' face, a countenance shaped by uncomfortable waiting in scratchy clothes, for what seems like an eternity, before the photographer's flash explodes into the back of the eye and lingers there, a ghost floating before everything the eye gazes upon. The mockingbird worried the air above Old Meja's lowered head. It plucked at the thin wisps of gray hair between her laced fingers as it swooped and looped back to its perch on the picture frame, as if it were gathering dross for its nest.

"Old Meja, listen," exclaimed Cesar.

The old woman raised her head slightly, to listen but avoid the stares of Maria and Louis. Faintly, a sound insinuated itself in the realm of her hearing. It was, at first, a thin sound, like the rustling of twigs heard beneath the rush and babble of a stream, but the sound grew stronger. As Old Meja strained to listen, the sound became familiar, and it took the shape of Papa's voice, calling out her name. The old woman peered between the gauzy legs of the phantoms looming over her and scarcely discerned the silhouette of her husband when he was young. From behind the swirling squall of shadows, Papa called, and Old Meja struggled to see him as if she were squinting through the crystalline substance of fifty years.

At that moment, Cesar recognized the tableau from his grandmother's memory. He saw how she cowered before Maria and Louis as Papa called from a distant shore.

"Old Meja," Cesar cried, "look up at your sister. Look up before it is too late."

Old Meja forced herself to lift her face to the grim ghost of her sister, and, as she did, Maria moved toward her, out of Louis' embrace. Old Meja flinched and clenched her quivering eyelids.

"Old Meja, open your eyes. Please, open your eyes."

The old woman, with an obvious force of will, opened her eyes to see Maria kneeling before her, offering her hand.

"No, no," sobbed Old Meja, "I cannot."

"Old Meja, take her hand."

Old Meja, trembling uncontrollably, slumped forward.

"Please leave me," she wept, over and over again.

Cesar knelt beside his grandmother and gently cradled her forearm with both of his hands. He tenderly raised her hand toward Maria's, but, before her hand was halfway up, Cesar felt Old Meja raise her arm out of his grasp, and, with her head still hung toward the floor, Old Meja finished raising her hand on her own.

Old Meja and Maria touched each other's fingers then joined their hands in a fond grasp.

At that instant, the cataclysm of shadows ceased. Cesar was alone in the silent room with the cold form of his grandmother. When he looked up at the photograph of Maria and Louis, he saw that the cameo pendant was gone. Outside, in the calm of the summer night, a mockingbird mimicked the red song of the cardinal.

The Scent of Baby Powder

C.J. twisted the key in the pitted brass padlock until it fell open, and then he removed it from the hasp. Grasping the edge of the splintery plank door, he tugged it open and scraped a quarter-circle in the dirt before the low, rough shed. As he peered into the deep shadow, he was cautious of the skittery rattles coming from under a jumble of old furniture piled by the rusty hulk of a tractor. A breath of arid, musty air exhaled from the gloom inside the shed, and, in a single ray of sunlight that pierced the tin roof, C.J. saw a cloud of dust-motes rise and eddy.

"C.J.!" shouted his father from the back porch, "quit standing there and get a place cleared out for this stuff!"

C.J. stepped into the dimness of the shed and gingerly lifted a stack of wicker baskets from the dusty shelf of a tumbled-down bookcase. As he turned to hunt for a place to set down his load, he felt something scurry down his right forearm. C.J. tossed the baskets in the air and furiously slapped at himself with both hands.

"The heck with this," C.J. muttered, and he scooted the fallen pile under a long table with his toe. He returned to the bookshelf and tipped a tangled coil of rope to the floor and kicked it underneath the table also. He did the same with the rest of the discarded household stuff, plastic flower pots, thin-soled work boots, boxes of his sister's old clothes, until the space beneath the table would hold no more.

C.J. bounded out of the shed, and the mid-morning sun blinded him. He squinted and shielded his eyes with a quick salute, and he was surprised when he heard a voice as he swung himself from the top porch-rail into the shade of the veranda.

"I don't know why your mother wants to keep this stuff," his father gruffly remarked and then turned and vanished into the house.

C.J. suddenly felt the nagging ebb of confusion sweep over him again. It was if he were living the dream he often had when things weren't right in the house, when his father withdrew into himself and shut out his family, the world. In C.J.'s dream, his father would be teaching him how to tie his shoes, just as he had many years before, except, in the dream, C.J. would tie a perfect bow on his first try, the loops even, the ends not too long or short, and his father would untie it and say, almost, son, try again, and his father would flash him an encouraging, hollow smile. In the dream, C.J. would tie perfect bows every time, and, every time, his father would untie it and say, almost, try again.

C.J. glanced down at the items neatly arranged on the porch, and the care with which they were placed belied his father's stern tone. These were the baby's things. His father had tenderly lined up the dismantled crib, the mobiles of bright, cloth clowns, the deflated walker, the johnny-jump-up, the tiny rocking chair. Beside these were a tidy row of boxes. One held bedding, another clothes. The last box in the row was full of stuffed animals. Everything was freshly washed and folded, C.J. knew, by his father. Everything smelled of the faint scent of baby powder.

"Go easy on him, C.J." his mother said.

C.J., startled, turned to see his mother on the bottom step of the stairs. Her eyes were rimmed with red again, and she still wore her housecoat.

"This took us all by surprise, son, and we all have to accept it in our own ways," she said, her voice trailing. "Are you okay?"

"Sure, Mom."

C.J. removed the boxes and other things from the porch to the shed, but, this time, he carefully arranged them on the bookshelf, heedless of the spiders and the fleeing mice.

C.J. dropped his bologna sandwich when he saw his father enter the kitchen dressed in his Highway Department uniform. His father had called in sick every morning for the last three weeks, including this morning. The telephone sat on a small table in the hall outside C.J.'s bedroom, and, even though it was summer vacation, C.J. had found himself waking at six o' clock every morning to listen for his father's voice. The first day his father had called, he had cried on the phone as he explained to Mr. Ross what had happened. C.J., listening from under the sheet in the warm dawn, had cried too.

This was when the confusing feeling had begun. C.J. had not cried at the funeral, not because he wasn't sad or that he didn't hurt inside, but because he was sixteen, and his two best friends were there. C.J.'s father hadn't cried at the funeral either. He had been a rock, grim-faced but solid as he comforted his sobbing wife and daughter. As C.J. had sat in the rickety folding chair at the grave-side, and listened to the endless monotone of the minister, the polite, stifled murmurs of grief, the drone of a plane as it had slowly crossed the sky, he had watched his father's granite endurance, and, at that moment, he wanted to be like his father in every way.

So, C.J. had realized, on that first morning when his father had called in to excuse himself, and the rich baritone of his voice had cracked in the stillness of the empty hallway, that the reason the back of his throat ached until he burst out with choked sobs was not that he had suppressed his grief for too long. C.J. wept because his father wept. And every morning since, as he listened to his father tersely identify himself and then simply say, 'not yet,' C.J. dreaded the moment when he might hear his father weep again.

"My, my, my," C.J.'s mother said, shaking C.J. from his thoughts, "don't we look dapper today?"

"What good is a man if he has no purpose?" his father replied and seated himself at the head of the table. "I don't guess I was put on this earth for no reason."

His voice caught, and he quickly turned to look out of the window. C.J. ducked his head under the table and pretended to look for bits of lettuce from his fallen sandwich. When he looked up again, he was relieved that his father busied himself with spreading mustard on a piece of rye bread.

"Ross called and said that a professor from the university is coming down to study the Manders' crossing. Ross thought I might like to help him out, detour traffic, chase off the rubberneckers, you know, pretend like I was doing something."

C.J.'s father smiled for the first time in months, and C.J. was doubly elated. First, it was good to see his eyes crinkle as the broad grin spread across his weathered face, and, second, anything to do with Manders' crossing aroused C.J.'s deep curiosity. Manders' crossing was the closest thing their town had to a famous or historic landmark. The crossing was simply a stretch of highway, no more than thirty yards long, that rose in a gentle, almost imperceptible, incline. The thing that made Manders' crossing unique, though, was the fact that, if a vehicle were left on that stretch of road, in neutral with the emergency brake off, the car would slowly roll uphill, pushed by unseen forces. Supposedly, that thousand square yards was a vortex of unimaginable magnetic fields, or, if you listened to the more excitable gossips around town, the doorway to another dimension.

"Can I come with you, Dad?" C.J. asked.

From the way his father locked him in his steady gaze, C.J. was afraid that the request, the added responsibility of keeping a watchful eye on him, might give his father a reason to call Mr. Ross back and excuse himself once again.

"Never mind, Dad, I..." C.J. quickly added.

"It's okay, son, I'd like you to come along."

His father smiled again.

As C.J. and his father pulled off the highway onto the gravel shoulder that flanked Manders' crossing, C.J. saw that the professor, and what must be an assistant, were already there. Parked beside the road was a green fleet car with the university emblem painted on the door, and behind it was a Chevy van with black plastic panels glued all the way around it from the bottom of the windows to a foot off the ground. The overall effect, C.J. thought, was that the van was wearing a black celluloid skirt, and he could not help but snicker.

"Be polite, son," his father said curtly, "I'll bet you end up learning something if you pay attention."

C.J. and his father walked from their truck to where the professor was standing with his arm outstretched.

"Hello, hello, I'm Dr. Snead." He shook both C.J.'s and his dad's hands vigorously. "And this is Mr. Cutrall. He's going to be helping me today."

Mr. Cutrall nervously extended his hand, and, after shaking, snatched it back. He was lanky with a beak-like nose and a mop of wild, black hair, the opposite of Dr. Snead's short obesity and balding white head.

"Well," C.J.'s father said after a long pause, "what can I do to help you today?"

"We'd like to start by taking a few soil samples from both sides of the road about every ten feet. We're going to set up some video equipment, and we're going to put the van on the road here, sort of as a guinea pig. So, if you could block traffic on either side of the railroad tracks for about fifty yards, we would appreciate it."

"About how long are you going to need the road blocked off? Anyone trying to get through is in for a mighty long detour."

"Oh, we'll be out of your way in a couple of hours. We've got to get back to the university before four."

C.J.'s father walked back to his truck and swung out a pair of orange-striped saw horses from the bed and planted them in the oncoming lanes fifty yards on either side of the tracks, but there was no traffic anywhere in sight. As he walked back to the vantage point of the front seat of his truck, Dr. Snead flagged him with a frantic wave of his arm and ran toward him.

"I almost forgot," panted Dr. Snead, "to ask you if you knew anything about the history of this place. When was the road built?"

C.J.'s father's face went white. C.J. felt nausea tugging at the pit of his stomach because he realized why Mr. Ross had asked his father to do this.

"It opened October thirteenth, nineteen-sixty-three," C.J.'s father replied softly, staring past Dr. Snead at a distant point on the horizon.

"That's quite a memory you've got there," Dr. Snead with a grin, "can you tell me how many cars have been over since then?"

"It was his birthday," C.J.'s father whispered, "his tenth birthday."

"Whose birthday? What are you talking about?" Dr. Snead's grin had vanished, and he was flushed all the way to the top of his bald head. Mr. Cutrall wandered up just then, holding a jar of dirt.

"My older brother's birthday. I was home sick that day. I made him a slingshot from a stick, and strips of an old inner tube, and a piece of the tongue of Dad's old work boot," C.J.'s father continued in a monotone, looking at no one.

"What's up? What is this all about?" blurted Mr. Cutrall.

The interruption snapped C.J.'s father from his distraction. He looked squarely at both of the men and resumed, this time in his strong, official Highway Department voice.

"On October thirteenth, nineteen-sixty-three, the afternoon of the opening of this railroad crossing, a school bus stalled on the tracks and was hit by the three-fifteen Southern Pacific from Dunsville. There were no survivors."

"Well," Mr. Cutrall chortled, "I guess things haven't always rolled off of the tracks by themselves."

Dr. Snead whirled on him and snatched the jar from his grasp. He caught hold of his bony arm and spun him around, motivating him toward the van with a thick forefinger insistently prodding his spine.

"My apologies," Dr. Snead said over his shoulder, "we'll hurry and get out of your way."

For an awful moment, C.J. was afraid his father was going to cry, and he looked away. But, when he could not help but look back, his father pulled his cap low over his eyes and exhaled slowly through pursed lips.

"Let's wait in the cab, son. I think these fellows are on a goose chase."

C.J. and his father watched the professor and his helper through the windshield of the truck as they scurried about, pulled up plugs of earth through the gravel, positioned video cameras on tripods, wrote in fluttering spiral notebooks. A car pulled up to the barricade, and the driver honked the horn and poked his head out of the window. C.J. and his father ambled over, and C.J.'s father explained the detour. His hand sliced left and right through the air as he described the proper route. The driver slowly nodded and, with C.J.'s father's assistance, backed up, turned around and vanished down the road.

As C.J. and his father crossed the tracks on their way back to the truck, Dr. Snead stopped the van alongside them and heaved himself out.

"What are those black sheets for?" asked C.J.

"Oh, well…they're, well, it would take a while to explain, son," Dr. Snead muttered and looked sheepishly at C.J.'s father.

"They are for studying magnetic fields," Mr. Cutrall chimed in, appearing from the other side of the van.

C.J. looked expectantly at his father. He stopped at the back of the van and half turned, his arms folded.

"We think that this phenomenon is caused by some sort of magnetic field caused by, perhaps, the confluence of these metal rails with the minerals in the ground. This field then reacts to the metal in a vehicle. We are going to dust these black sheets with a white powder mixed with fine steel particles. If there is some magnetic field causing the van to move, then, hopefully, the video cameras will record the movements of these fields as they reveal themselves by the patterns formed in the steel particles mixed with the white powder."

With that explanation spat out, Mr. Cutrall furiously rubbed the plastic sheets, which charged them with static electricity, then generously powdered them with an old flour sifter. He continued in this manic fashion until he circled the van and finished by C.J.'s side again.

"There. Let's see what happens."

But nothing happened. The three of them, C.J., Mr. Cutrall and Dr. Snead, stood shoulder to shoulder at the side of the van, while C.J.'s father watched them from off of the tracks. They waited for long minutes, but the van stood motionless. The still air was filled with the scent of baby powder.

Then, far off, and very faintly, they heard the plaintive wail of a train whistle. The van, at that instant, rocked forward and slowly rolled up the hill. C.J., shocked, turned to his father, and his father stared at the powdered sheets on the back of the van. Tears streamed down his face. He was smiling.

The automatic zooms of the video cameras slowly turned in unison as the van crept past C.J., and he saw, on the back panels, the disruption of the white powder in the shape of small hand prints, thirty, forty of them rise dark out of the white powder, the hand prints of children.

The Rattler's Tale

Ragged clouds passed from in front of the full moon as Raven slid from the shadows of the rocks into the clearing before the cave mouth. She froze in the sudden, wan light and listened intently, her head cocked, her eyes darting from shadow to shadow. Her stance was so motionless she seemed inanimate. In the feeble light that washed over the barrenness of the desert, she might have been a young Joshua tree. Then, on the farthest fringe of her hearing, she detected the frail rasp of scales on sand. Her still shadow stretched across the desert floor to where the boulders piled atop one another in the darkness, and, from out of her shadow's head, she saw a subtle movement. Raven strained to decipher the vague motion, but it was difficult, like watching a ropy wisp of smoke rise into heavy mist. Just as she realized what this mirage was, it glided across her bare foot and wound itself into a thick coil. The viper flicked its tongue in and out of the triangular wedge of its head as it scrutinized the corners of the night. Raven smiled.

"You can stand guard for me, Long One," she whispered, "in case they return before I am finished."

In immediate obedience, the serpent raised up as if to strike, its forked tongue busy as it tasted the shadows that ringed the clearing. Raven groped her way into the blackness of the cave entrance, and she remained silent, even when she barked her shin on an upturned wooden box. She reached down and ran her nimble fingers over the provisions scattered on a low makeshift table. Working as if she were blind, she discovered the odd details that filled the meager spare time of the miners: the rough corncob of a homemade pipe, the pungent suede of a tobacco pouch, the delicate filigree of a pocket watch, a necklace strung with rough beads, the cold, crimped roundness of blasting caps, a large hairy ball. Raven snatched back her hand. Very slowly she extended her fingertips back toward the thing. She almost giggled out loud as her touch ferreted out the meaning of the hairy object. It was the knotted, frayed end of a thick rope. She continued her sightless search of the table top until her hand brushed against the nearly weightless cube of the matchbox. Beside it she felt the cool glass globe of the lantern.

With the lantern lighted, she turned to survey the rest of the rude shelter. Three crude beds had been fashioned from knotty planks supported by powder kegs. Straw spilled out of lumpy burlap mattresses. A tattered sheet covered the opening that led deeper into the mine. As Raven drew nearer, she could see, in the flickering light, that the sheet was printed with tiny bouquets of roses. She took a deep breath and threw back the curtain. The shaft sloped steeply down from where she stood and was supported by huge timbers. There were so many hewn beams lining the passageway that Raven fancied these men had tunneled into a mountain of oak. Deep within the splintery corridor she could hear the echoes of the pops and creaks as the mountain settled down on the wooden supports. When she turned back to the cave opening, fine sand sifted down into her hair.

Raven went to each of the kegs which supported the rude beds and rapped them with her knuckles, but they all rang hollow. She overturned the table and a stack of crates which served as a bureau as she searched for blasting powder. She kicked over a rocking chair and, with a great sweep of her arm, littered the cave floor with the pipe, tobacco, watch and necklace. But, as she watched these paltry treasures scatter onto the floor, she realized that the necklace was not strung with beads, but with human teeth. Raven ripped down the rose-printed sheet and stomped it into the dirt. Her eyes welled with tears as she trampled the sheet, but, as she spun with the lantern at arm's length, she glimpsed a small barrel tucked between the timbers a few yards down the shaft. She knelt beside the cask, and, as she tried to pull it into the open, a pungent liquid sloshed onto her hand. Raven gingerly held her fingers to her nose and recognized the acrid smell of kerosene. Placing the lantern outside the cave, she returned and wrestled the keg up and splashed the wooden walls of the passageway. She continued to spatter the walls as she slowly backed out of the corridor, and she emptied the barrel on the primitive bedding.

Raven withdrew from the reeking confines of the cave to where the rattlesnake lay coiled at attention. A breeze had lifted through the rocks, and the cool wind refreshed her although the cloying stench of kerosene still clung, and she could feel her skin beginning to burn under her damp shirt. She grasped the lantern and, without hesitation, lofted it deep into the cavern. It burst in the throat of the shaft, and flames raced out toward her the way that, in still water, a wave rings out from the place a pebble has broken the surface and gone under. A blast of heat blew past her as the flames halted at the cave mouth and clawed angrily at the desert night. Raven staggered back a few steps and shielded her face with her arm. It was if some enraged mythical beast were howling fire from the blaze of its lair.

Raven turned her back on the inferno and gazed out into the desert below the rocks, but she could see nothing because the fire still burned in her retinas. The after-image, the ghost, of the flames floated through the blackness even though the sky had cleared and the moon was bright. The rattlesnake skimmed past her ankles and spiraled himself into a sentry position. Raven stared at the place, just below the cave mouth, below the jumbled boulders, where her father rested. As the specter of the fire faded from her vision, she began to see the wooden poles of the sacred platforms, bleached bone white in the fullness of the moon. The spindly staves held up, toward the sky, the remains of the great men and women of her tribe. These platforms were their eternal berths, their memorials, the places where they could finally speak with their fathers and their father's fathers. Here they rejoined the circular spirit of the earth, neither young nor old, strong nor feeble, cunning nor simple. Here they became one with the land and the sky and the waters. They transformed into spirit, like the wind or the morning mists that caressed the face of the world.

Raven knew that her father was here because he was a great artist with the skins of snakes. He alone had been able to craft the narrow hides into scabbards and sheaths and ceremonial covers for the hallowed long pipes.

Many chiefs had sought his talent for fashioning the rattling ornaments for their war bonnets. They knew that her father would only use the longest rattles from the oldest snakes so that when the chiefs danced around the harvest fires the children would run to their mothers to get their feet out of the sand.

Raven remembered the way her father would wait, hunkered near the hole of a snake nest for hours, gently singing his prayer for the spirit of the snake that burrowed there. When the rattler would finally emerge, her father would respectfully ask permission from the serpent to use his skin, and then thank the snake as he gently cradled the reptile, still alive, into his leather bag. No one had ever seen how her father would kill the snakes, not even Raven nor her mother, and, when asked, her father would only smile and speak of the nobility and courage of the rattlesnake. As her father had lay dying, he had called Raven to his side and told her, ÔThe rattlesnake has taken good care of me in my lifetime. They will take care of you as well. Do not be afraid, and they will be your companions. They will protect you.'

Raven felt the familiar, long stroke of the silky dry scales as the rattler glided past her bare instep. She turned back to the blaze and was satisfied when she heard a coaling timber snap. From out of the mine came a shower of fist-sized embers and a roiling cloud of dust. She could hear the rumble of boulders collapsing into the shaft. Turning back to face the refreshing breeze, Raven again saw the after-image of the flames scour the center of wherever she looked, but there seemed to be more flames, shaped differently, thin and spiky, dancing up from a hard ball of fire, when she gazed again at the burial ground. As the mirage of flame faded from her sight, she realized she was seeing a different fire, a real fire, two real fires moving shakily up through the hallowed biers of her ancestors. Raven could now hear, above the flapping crackle of the cave-fire, the panting grunts of three men as they scrambled up the rocks toward the cave. The rattlesnake twitched and jerked between her feet, first in one direction and then another.

A man stumbled from between the boulders to Raven's left, much nearer than she expected. In the wild, flickering light of the fire and the torch he waved before him, she could see the savage squint of his eyes, the matted path of drool which coursed from the corner of his mouth down his long, dirty beard. She feinted as if to run past the man, but he spread his arms wide and brandished his torch.

"Silas! Samuel! Lookee here," the man cackled, "I think I caught me a fire-bug. Let's see..."

The man went silent the second he saw the rattler coiled between Raven's feet. He stood perfectly still with his mouth opening and closing, as if he were trying to speak. He began to take a step backward, but, before his hind foot had even a chance to touch the ground, the snake had propelled itself toward him through the clearing, a diamondback arrow. The rattler's head hit the man at the place where his beard met his chest, and the force of the strike thrust the fangs up under the beard to the pale flesh of the throat. The miner threw his hands into the air and staggered in a circle. His head twitched back and forth. The rattler looked like a writhing necktie as the man fell backward and began to convulse in rapid spasms.

Raven did not have a chance to flee over the shuddering form of the stricken miner before the second man leaped from between two boulders and clamped her arm above the elbow with an iron grip. Raven spun to loosen herself from his hold, and the vigor of her action threw him off balance. He pulled her to the ground with him as he fell before the blazing mouth of the cave. As the man struggled to his feet, still gripping Raven's arm, the rattler struck him in the right eye. With the man's horrified face nearly in her own as they wrestled in the sand, Raven could see how the rattlesnake's fangs had entered the flesh above the eyebrow and exited in the crepey skin of the eyelid. The man grappled with the serpent, his both hands not large enough to go all the way around the rattler where he gripped its middle, and he finally, with a strength induced by panic, ripped the snake from his brow. Blinded by blood and venom, he lurched sideways, his fists covering his eyes until he careened headlong into the licking flames of the mine.

Raven staggered to her feet and stumbled across the clearing as hideous shrieks from the cave's inferno echoed through the night. Raven was nearly to a notch between the rocks that ringed the clearing when a heavy weight fell on her from behind. Her breath knocked out of her, she impotently struggled to wriggle from beneath the third miner. He was a huge man, fat and sweaty, and his beard felt like a tumbleweed as it scratched her cheek. Raven managed to turn over, but her legs were still pinned beneath his massive chest. His hot, whiskey-fraught breath panted in her face, and he grinned wildly at her, his eyes small and close-set, the eyes of a pig. The screams from the flames had ceased, and Raven heard the familiar, dizzily frenzied sizzle of the snake's rattle.

The obese miner heard it too. He scrambled around with his back to the rocks and hugged Raven in front of him. She was a ridiculously small shield for his filthy girth, but he also wore a pair of furry chaps, and he pulled his knees up so that his shins, and the hairy hide that covered them, hid them from a direct strike. Between the fat man's knees, Raven could see the rattler sway back and forth, looking for a place to sink his fangs into the corpulent flesh. For what seemed like an aching eternity in the flickering light of the clearing, the snake swayed as the miner huddled against the rocks, keeping Raven between himself and the undulating serpent. The rattler struck with a speed and ferocity which surprised even Raven. Instinctively, the fat miner brought up his huge knees to shield his face, and the snake, its elastic jaw unhinged wide, bit down into the woolly leather of the miner's chaps. The rattler sank its hollow, venomous fangs as deeply as it could, but the leather was thick and the wool heavy. The death-bite could not penetrate the chaps, and worse, Raven realized as the rattler writhed helplessly, his fangs were embedded in the leather like an axe in a green log. The fat man unsheathed his long knife and brought it down on the snake in one fluid movement. The first slash sliced into the rattler's spine. Then the knife-blade severed ribs and entrails in a razor-sharp sweep again and again. The last slash rent the shredded body from the rattler's head, still stuck tight in the leather of the leggings. As the headless carcass writhed on the ground by the miner's boot, Raven, for the first time, cried out.

The fat man kicked open the door of the cabin and heaved Raven inside, sending her tumbling against the stone hearth. She bumped her head on the front ledge, and, when she raised both her hands, bound with a rawhide thong, to her forehead, she felt the sticky dampness of blood. The miner slammed the door shut, and the inside of the room was as dark as a cave. Raven heard his wheezing pant coming closer and closer to her in the darkness. Then he stopped. Raven jerked her head from the sudden brightness of a match being struck, and , in the sputtering light, she saw his jowls tighten from his toothless grin as he lit the kerosene lamp on the mantle. He flicked the match, still lit, from between his thumb and forefinger at Raven, and it bounced off of the damp leather of her shirt. As she frantically stamped out the match and slapped at her chest, the fat man cackled.

He ambled to the table in the center of the room and slumped heavily into a rickety chair. Wheezing, he shucked off the chaps and pulled one foot up onto his knee and tugged the boot off of his dirty bare foot. Raven watched him without blinking as he tugged off the other boot and arranged both of them carefully beside the table. The air in the tiny cabin began to stink.

"So, you thought you could burn us out, huh?" the fat man chortled. "You thought that we'd see all that mess and just decide to pack up and leave forever."

The fat man leaned back in the chair and squinted at Raven with one eye. He loosened the leather tie on a pouch he carried slung below his huge waist and raised the flap, resting his hand inside.

"I think you got it all wrong, Baby Injun. I think all you did was get yourself into a heap of trouble."

From the pouch he pulled out a corncob pipe and a leather tobacco pouch. He placed them carefully on the table.

"What did we do to put you on the war path, Pocahontas?"

With a great effort, he crossed his legs and scratched the dirty yellow sole of his foot.

"Was it that pitiful bone-yard up there by the claim you was protecting?"

He slipped his hand back into the pouch and retrieved another necklace strung with human teeth.

"These are all I ever took. Just pick up a skull and shake it real hard. These teeth just fall out like seed corn out of a basket. These funny-lookin' Injun teeth."

"You disrespect the honored ones, their spirit," Raven hissed as she blinked back hot tears.

"You disrespect me, little girl, and you're going to be sorry you ever did that."

Raven spit at the fat man and then raised both bound hands to wipe spittle from her chin. The miner chuckled softly and slipped hid hand back into the pouch.

"You're too feisty for your own good. You got nothing protecting you now."

The fat man slowly slid his hand out of the pouch and held it out toward Raven so that she could see what rested in his palm.

"You see. Nothing."

In the wavering light of the kerosene lamp Raven saw the head of the rattler, its jaws spread wide in its fatal attempt to pierce the leather of the chaps.

"What's he see now, Pocahontas? Let me put him up here so he can see what I'm going to do to you."

The fat man carefully placed the wide-jawed skull on the edge of the table, arranging it so that the dull eyes looked at the place where she lay in front of the hearth.

"I don't want to disrespect his..."

The fat man went silent and glanced abruptly over his shoulder. Raven listened too. On the farthest fringe of her hearing she detected the frail rasp of scales on sand. The fat man reached for the knife in his belt and unsheathed it.

"Spirit," Raven whispered, finishing the fat man's sentence.

"Shh..."

The fat man sat up straight and half-turned in the chair. Another sound faintly insinuated itself in the predawn stillness of the room. The sound was small, but it seemed to be coming from every direction. It was a distant sizzle, like a swarm of cicadas heard from across an open field. The fat man cocked his head, his eyes going wide. The sizzle grew louder, frenzied, until it sounded as though a hundred angry rattlers plagued the dirt surrounding the cabin. The fat man sprang to his feet, nearly upsetting the table. The pipe, tobacco, and the rattler's head were toppled from their careful arrangement on the table top.

The fat man paced the room, listening in one corner and then another. Raven frantically studied the floorboards for the place where the rattler's head had fallen, but it was nowhere to be seen. The fat man nervously passed the knife from one hand to the other as he strode from the door to the table and back again. The dizzying sizzle of a thousand rattles glutted the room. The fat man held his palms to his ears, and his mouth worked open and shut, in a soundless scream. A terrified field mouse scurried across the floor of the cabin, over the fat man's bare foot. Unnerved, the fat man snatched up one boot and thrust it on.

The seething racket ceased. The room once again was deadly hushed. Raven, bewildered, looked up at the stricken grimace contorting the fat man's face. He fell back into the chair, and, with agonizing slowness, tenderly slid the brogan from his bare foot. There, from where it had fallen into the boot, was the rattler's head, the fangs sunk their full length into the flesh of the fat man's heel.

A Simple Act of Kindness

It was a Friday morning in September, and Peter had only been a crossing guard for three weeks, but he was already accustomed to the routine which brought him to school forty-five minutes earlier than his friends. His mom dropped him off at the school, and he went around the building to the janitor's room, the only door unlocked that early. As he pulled open the metal door, he stifled a cough from the overwhelmingly clean stench of disinfectants and detergents. Peter crossed the room to the back wall where, on coat hooks, hung the orange plastic sashes which all of the crossing guards wore. Stan and Molly were already there, adjusting the belts and straps over their sweaters.

"Hey, hey, if it isn't Mr. Wisdom's little helper," Stan joked, "the little man's little man."

"Shut up, man," Peter replied, "you're just jealous because you're stuck at the kindergarten gate."

"I'd rather ride herd on rugrats than rub elbows with that spooky old dwarf."

"Really, Pete," Molly said, "I'm all the way on the other side of the playground, but when I watch him staring through the fence, it gives me the creeps."

"He's harmless, you bunch of babies. All he does is just stand there. He shows up right at seven forty-five, he never talks, he never bothers anybody, and, right on the stroke of eight, he picks up his bag and scurries back down the alley."

"I don't know," Stan said, rolling his eyes, "you ever see what he carries around in that bag?"

"Just some rags and stuff, some baby books."

"My dad says that once, when he was a kid, him and some of his friends found out where Mr. Wisdom stayed down in that alley. He says that they went down there one afternoon and caught him napping between some garbage cans. He says that they started going through the bag, to see if the dwarf was really like an old eccentric millionaire or something, see if maybe it was filled with hundred dollar bills or treasure or something. But," Stan paused, "guess what they found down at the bottom?"

"What?" Peter snorted, "some rags and baby books?"

"A head. An old woman's head. It was all dried up and the hair was falling out. He says it's the head of Wisdom's mother. He says that Mr. Wisdom cut it off to get even with her for making him a freak."

"Gotta go," Molly said without looking back. She hit the metal door running and disappeared around the corner.

"What a load of crap."

"You don't believe it?" Stan asked, a wicked smile spreading across his face.

"No way. He'd be in jail."

"Man, even the cops are too afraid to look in that bag."

"Yeah, right."

"Well, that's how I heard it. Anyway, if I were you, I think I'd stay away from that bag. No telling what he might do if you happened to see that head."

"I'll keep that in mind," Peter said sarcastically.

"Well, it's that time. Let's go guard the kiddies."

"You go on ahead," Peter said, looking around the room, "I've got to find another stop sign. A screw's loose in the handle of mine."

"I'll keep that in mind," Stan said as he smirked from the doorway.

Peter glanced down at his watch. Seven forty-five. The morning was still and somber because the sky was heavy with gray rain clouds. Maybe, he thought, the old man has something else to do today. But, as he looked back up, he saw Mr. Wisdom step out of the alleyway and trot across the street. He wore a long, military-issue trench coat which drug the ground, and the sleeves were rolled up into huge wads around his wrists. Underneath this he wore a dingy white tee shirt and an oversized pair of dress trousers which were held up at his waist with a rope and were rolled up so much at the bottom that the cuffs looked like link sausages hula-hooping around his ankles. He wore a pair of stereo headphones around his neck, attached to nothing, like some futuristic necklace. Peter studied the bag Mr. Wisdom carried hugged against his chest and noticed that the bottom did have a sort of roundness to it. On the side, near the bottom, Peter thought he saw, even from a distance, a greasy stain soaked through the paper. Mr. Wisdom sat the bag down on the sidewalk, as he did every morning, and gripped the chain link with both hands, pressing his nose through one space in the diamond pattern, his eyes lined up with two other spaces so that his view was unobstructed by the wire. Mr. Wisdom stood at the corner of the fence and watched the children converge on the playground from the surrounding neighborhoods and play, and laugh, and call out to one another. He peered through the chain link like an animal at the zoo, curious about this strange world of people.

Peter returned his attention to his post at the crosswalk where a group of third-graders waited for his consent to cross over to the school yard. Peter walked into the middle of the crosswalk with his stop sign, even though there was no automobile traffic, and waved the kids across. As he stepped back up onto the curb on the far side of the street, he heard a shout from near the corner where Mr. Wisdom kept his silent watch. Peter whirled around and saw Kenny James and his buddies, Fred and Rusty, leaping and jumping down the sidewalk in the direction of the dwarf. Peter was surprised to see them coming to school from this way. One reason Peter tolerated his post on the nearly deserted street behind the school was that he was unlikely to run into this threesome.

Kenny and his two cronies were playing soccer with a stone as they rough-housed down the sidewalk toward Mr. Wisdom. Two of them would try to prevent the third from kicking the rock down the sidewalk, and, when the stone was finally kicked through, two would gang up on whomever got to the stone first. Mr. Wisdom kept his vigil at the fence, totally heedless of the rough-and-tumble play careening toward him. Kenny tripped up Fred as they jockeyed for position around the rock, and, barely missing Fred's ear with his combat boot, kicked the stone right between Mr. Wisdom's feet. The tiny man stood as if he were a statue, even as the three boys wrestled and fought one another over his back, their feet dicing between his to extricate the smooth stone. They fell against each other and Mr. Wisdom as he simply clung to the chain link, the wire pressed deeply into the flesh between his eyes. Kenny, with a final, desperate kick, succeeded in both dislodging the stone from between Mr. Wisdom's feet and toppling Mr. Wisdom's bag so that the contents spilled out across the sidewalk.

Mr. Wisdom whirled on them, his jaw working with a soundless ferocity. The three boys froze, suddenly aware of the dwarf's furious indignation, until the sound he uttered caught up with the twitching of his face.

"H–h–h–h–hey–hey–hey–hey," Mr. Wisdom stuttered, his cracked voice bleating the persistent syllable.

Mr. Wisdom fell to his knees and frantically crawled after the rags and books which Kenny and his friends now scattered with menacing glee. As Mr. Wisdom scrambled after handfuls of bright rags, Kenny retoppled the bag and threw fistfuls of cloth scraps skyward, letting them rain down like giant confetti.

Peter suddenly found his legs propelling him across the street to the corner at top speed.

"That's enough," Peter screamed as he threw himself on Kenny.

The force of Peter's lunge rolled them into the fence, and, as they scuffled to get up, Peter banged the back of his head into Kenny's nose. Instantly, blood streamed down, and he stepped back and gingerly dabbed at his lip with the back of his hand.

"You're gonna pay," Kenny muttered as he wiped a crimson streak along the back of his forearm.

Kenny motioned for his buddies to follow him around the corner, and all three of them sullenly stalked up the sidewalk to the school entrance, Kenny holding his head back and pinching the bridge of his nose. Mr. Wisdom still anxiously retrieved the rags and spine-broken picture books, oblivious to the departure of the bullies or Peter's trembling figure as he fell to his knees and began warily returning the scraps into the righted paper bag.

It took a few minutes for the pair of them to refill the bag, and, when Peter had cautiously placed the last shred into the sack, he looked up to see Mr. Wisdom staring directly into his eyes.

"There you go," Peter mumbled nervously.

Mr. Wisdom said nothing, but continued to intently observe Peter as he rose from his knees and retreated a few small steps.

"They're gone now. I'll tell the principal what they did. You'll be okay."

Mr. Wisdom only stared deeper. Peter noticed a small trickle of blood from Mr. Wisdom's right eyebrow, and, as he stared at it, Mr. Wisdom slowly raised his hand and wiped it away.

"Okay, I've got to get back to my post. Be seeing you."

Peter lowered his head and turned back in the direction of the crossing when he heard a clear, strong voice behind him.

"Thank you."

Peter spun around to see Mr. Wisdom standing on the sidewalk, the bag clutched in his short arms.

"Don't loiter after school today," Mr. Wisdom said, and he stepped into the street and crossed over to the alley where he disappeared behind a dumpster.

Peter looked down at his wristwatch. It was eight 'o clock.

"You're kidding me," Stan said.

"No, really," Peter insisted, "he spoke to me. He said, 'Don't loiter after school today,' and then he left."

The two boys unstrapped their sashes and carefully hung them on the coat hooks.

"How did he say it?" Stan asked, "Did he say it mean, like he was threatening you or something?"

"No. He said it really plain and nice. It sounded like he was trying to do me a favor ."

"A favor? He was probably telling you to stay away from him or he'd make sure you didn't tell anyone about what happened."

"No way. It was like he was trying to help me out somehow."

"I don't know," Stan said thoughtfully, "did you see what was in the bottom of the bag?"

"Rags and books, you moron, just like I told you this morning."

"No head?"

"No head."

"What do you think Kenny is going to do?"

"Well, all he said was, 'You're gonna pay.' I think he's going to try to beat me up."

"Brilliant deduction, Sherlock. Did he say when?"

"No. I'm just going to watch out for him. I don't think he'd try to fight me while I was on crosswalk duty."

"Probably not," Stan agreed, "but, if I were you, I'd watch out during lunch tomorrow and on the way home. Are you going to tell Mr. Patterson about what happened?"

"I tried to this morning, right after duty, but he was busy with this new kid. Old Lady Robinson wouldn't let me see him."

"Hmm, maybe Kenny'd go easy on you if you just forgot about it."

"I don't know, Stan. I really hate that guy. Ever since he stole my gym uniform out of my locker and broke my glasses when I tried to get it back."

"He might break more than your glasses this time."

"I don't care," Peter blurted, "I'm really sick of him."

Peter sat on his hands on a hard, wooden chair in the long hallway outside of Mr. Patterson's office. He shifted his weight from one arm to the other, but the chair was impossibly uncomfortable. As he wriggled, he upset his book pack from where he had hung it on the back of the chair, and it fell to the polished floor in the empty hallway with startling bang. Mrs. Robinson poked her head around the corner from where she sat at her desk. She tilted her head back so she could see Peter through her bifocals which had slid down her pointy nose. Her hair was brilliantly white, and she turned her head back and forth, first looking at Peter through one eye and then the other. Peter watched her expectantly, a nervous knot hardening in his stomach. She looked like a giant, inquisitive rat.

"Are you still here, Peter," she nasally keened in the emptiness of the hallway.

"Yes, ma'am. I need to speak with Mr. Patterson."

"Well," she said, drawing out the syllable as if she doubted his request were possible, "let me go in and see if he will be available today."

Peter watched her slide past the door she opened just enough to allow herself through, but he still caught a glimpse of Mr. Patterson sitting idly behind his huge desk, staring absently out of the window. She closed the door behind her, and, after a few minutes of muffled voices on the other side of the door, she reappeared.

"Mr. Patterson is going to be busy for a while longer, Peter. Can you tell me what this is all about, so that maybe I can help you?"

"No, Mrs. Robinson."

"It's nearly four. If you come in tomorrow right after you finish with your crosswalk duty, I'll try to make sure you see him then."

"Okay," Peter mumbled.

"Run along home, now, before your mother gets worried."

Peter picked up his book pack and trudged down the long hallway to where the afternoon light dimly shone through the glass window of the exit door. Peter peered out the window, trying to see if anybody was waiting outside, and he noticed that it had begun to lightly rain. Peter pulled the collar of his jacket up around his neck and raised the book pack over his head as a makeshift umbrella. He pushed open the door with his foot and ran down the stone steps. He turned right and jogged along the side of the building, and, when he got to the tall bush at the corner of the building, he turned right again and collided head-on with Kenny James coasting on his bicycle. The mishap threw Kenny over the handlebars and knocked Peter flat on his back in the middle of the sidewalk. As Peter lay there, his eyelids fluttering from the rain falling in his face, he was aware of two more bicycles skidding up to within inches of his legs, and then he saw the faces of Rusty and Fred grinning down at him.

"Welly, welly, well," Fred chortled as he planted his boot on the wet sidewalk by Peter's ear, "look who's still hanging around so late."

"Yeah," said Rusty, placing the toe of his shoe on the point of Peter's jacket collar, pinning it to the ground, "we figured you'd have run home right after you finished your sissy job at the crosswalk."

Peter lay motionless, shallowly panting from having the wind knocked out of him, and he heard Kenny's voice approach from over his head.

"We weren't planning on beating the crap out of you until tomorrow, snitch," Kenny muttered.

Peter tried to roll over, but he was trapped by his pinned collar. Kenny sauntered around and straddled Peter then sat down heavily on his chest.

"I didn't tell Mr. Patterson anything. Really."

"Is that so, snitch?" Kenny said, bending down his head within a foot of Peter's.

"Really. He was busy all afternoon, and he didn't have time to see me."

"Oh, so. you were going to tell, but he didn't have time for you."

"No. No. I mean, as I was just leaving, I heard Old Lady Robinson tell someone that."

"Sure, snitch. How come you stuck up for the dwarf, man. He someone special to you? Who is that crazy runt? Your dad?"

Fred and Rusty cackled at the joke, and Kenny leaned back, laughing, his weight crushing Peter's sore stomach.

"Well, we can understand a kid sticking up for his own retarded dad, snitch. Fred, hand me his backpack."

Kenny got up from his seat on Peter's chest and took Peter's pack, ripping open the top and peering inside.

"Anything good for us today?"

Peter lay on the wet ground, motionless. He wished Kenny would punch him in the face, or kick him in the stomach, anything, just to get it over with.

"Nothing but trash, as far as I can see," Kenny stated and emptied the contents of Peter's pack into a puddle, "there, we cleaned it all out for you."

Peter closed his eyes and waited for them to leave. Suddenly, he felt a sharp jolt in his side, and he opened his eyes to see Kenny standing over him, his leg drawn back to kick again.

"Don't ever mess with me or my friends, snitch, or we'll make sure that you started looking like your daddy, the freak."

Peter closed his eyes at the second blow to his ribs and curled up on his side, the cold rain, falling harder now, soaking through the denim of his jeans. He waited for another kick, but, instead, he heard Kenny's voice grow fainter as the three boys picked up their bikes and walk them down the side of the building. Peter lay quietly until their voices receded in the distance, and then he heard another voice, but this one, he knew, was only in his mind. He heard Mr. Wisdom's voice, surprisingly clear and strong, utter the same sentence he had said that morning, Don't loiter after school today, Don't loiter after school today, until Mr. Wisdom's voice went silent also, and all he could hear was the pelting of the rain on the concrete sidewalk.

One week before Christmas, Peter stood in the bitter wind blowing down the deserted street behind the school and thrust his gloved hands deep into the pockets of his parka. He looked across the street and knew that it was seven forty-five, because Mr. Wisdom trotted with his odd, short-legged gait from the alley to the schoolyard fence. Peter had wondered if Mr. Wisdom might acknowledge their acquaintance after the Kenny incident by waving from his watch at the fence corner, or maybe crossing the street at Peter's post, exchanging pleasantries as he trotted by, or maybe even standing with Peter at the crosswalk to watch the children as they frolicked on the playground, but three months had gone by, and Mr. Wisdom had not once shown the slightest sign that he even knew Peter stood there wondering across the street. Every day, the old dwarf appeared out of the alley at seven forty-five, like a bizarre cuckoo emerging from its door in the clock, watched the children, and then promptly disappeared at eight.

Today, Peter could not help but notice, as he studied the old man from across the street, that Mr. Wisdom's trench coat was threadbare across his back, over his hunched shoulders, and that his hands were as red as lobster claws as he clenched the frosty chain link. When the wind died between frigid gusts, Peter could hear the fence rattle against the metal posts from Mr. Wisdom's tight grip as he shivered. In the calm, Mr. Wisdom's breath rose in a vaporous wreath around his head, but, when the icy wind blasted down the empty street, it tore his breath away, and there was no sign that Mr. Wisdom was even a living man and not the husk of a scarecrow clinging to the fence.

Peter, again, in spite of himself, found his legs stiffly carrying him across the street to the corner where the old man stood. He stopped about ten feet from Mr. Wisdom and slowly pulled his thick scarf out from around his neck and his parka hood.

"Here," Peter said, much more loudly than he had intended, and he waved the muffler at arm's length toward Mr. Wisdom.

Mr. Wisdom said nothing. He didn't look over his shoulder to see who was yelling at him. He didn't move at all from his watch at the fence, but it wasn't as if Mr. Wisdom were ignoring Peter so much as it seemed that Mr. Wisdom lived in a world in which Peter were unrecognizable, a parallel reality where crossing guards were merely mechanical servants trained to assist in the marvelous spectacle of children playing on a playground.

"You can have this to keep warm. I have another one at home," Peter said as he hesitantly walked closer to Mr. Wisdom, still waving the thick scarf.

Still, Mr. Wisdom remained motionless except for the occasional shiver which would start in his knees and rise up through his back to his shoulders and arms and end in a faint metallic rattle of chain link against steel post.

"Please take it. I can see you shivering from all the way across the street."

When Mr. Wisdom continued to stand there, oblivious to Peter's nervous entreaties, Peter exhaled a huge frosty breath, half in exasperation and half in apprehension, and stepped up behind Mr. Wisdom and warily placed the scarf around his trembling shoulders.

Peter immediately took two quick steps back and said, "You keep it. I want you to have it. It's really getting cold."

Peter continued to walk backward until he stumbled off the curb into the street, but Mr. Wisdom remained motionless at the fence.

Peter turned to cross back to his post at the crosswalk when he heard the strong, clear voice call to him from the corner. Peter whirled around to see Mr. Wisdom facing him.

"Thank you," said Mr. Wisdom.

The muffler was pulled tight around his collar and up over his ears and tied under his chin.

"You're welcome. If you want..." Peter began.

"At the assembly today, don't stand under the bleachers," Mr. Wisdom said as he bent down to pick up his bag.

"Don't stand under the bleachers?" Peter asked, puzzled, "There's no assembly today."

But Mr. Wisdom had already crossed the street and disappeared down the windy alley. Of course, it was eight o'clock.

As Peter sat at his desk in Mrs. Whybrew's class and absently gazed out of the window at a pair of starlings hunched into black knots on a swaying branch, the intercom at the front of the room crackled, and the classroom windows rattled from the amplified squeal of Mr. Patterson clearing his throat.

"Good morning, students," Mr. Patterson's voice boomed from the small box on the wall, "I have an announcement concerning the scheduling of a special assembly in the auditorium this morning."

Peter felt the skin on the back of his neck tighten, and all of his tiny neckhairs stood up and tingled.

"Because of the added security needed for the governor's visit to our city this weekend, Deputy Dogue has come to give his safety talk today instead of Friday. We will be leaving our classrooms to fill the auditorium..."

As Mr. Patterson droned on about assembly procedure, Peter slowly turned in his seat toward Stan, who sat two desks behind him. That morning, as soon as Peter had returned to the janitor's room after morning duty, he had told Stan what Mr. Wisdom had said. Now, Stan sat at his desk with his eyes fixed, his mouth hanging open and his face deathly pale.

"Stan!" Peter whispered under the monotone of Mr. Patterson's instructions, "Stan!"

Stan shook himself out of his stupor and focused on Peter.

"This is too weird," he whispered back.

Students were already leaving their desks to line up at the classroom door, and Peter and Stan hesitantly joined the end of the line. They silently trooped down the hall to the auditorium, and just as they stepped into the huge room, they both stopped.

"Where are you going to sit?" Stan asked Peter.

Peter only stared under the bleachers.

"The usual?" Stan inquired uneasily.

Peter continued to stand soundlessly, peering into the gloom of the metal mazework beneath the tall bleachers. The usual was the top row in the corner, and, when Mrs. Whybrew wasn't looking, a climb down the back of the bleachers so that they could sit on the hardwood floor with their backs against the cool concrete block wall, relaxing in the shadows under the highest seats.

"No way," Peter whispered.

"I'm not sitting down here in the front row with the first graders, prediction of doom or not," Stan muttered impatiently. "At least let's sit on the top in the middle."

Peter looked at the uppermost seats in the middle of the bleachers. A massive steel I-beam that supported the corrugated ceiling was bolted to the block wall just above the seats in the center of the bleachers. The beam was so low that Peter's father, during the Christmas concert the year before, had banged his head on it when he stood up to videotape Peter playing trombone in the band.

"Maybe we could jump up and grab that beam if the bleachers fell," Peter offered.

"C'mon, c'mon, the assembly is about to begin."

Peter and Stan clambered up the bleachers to the spot by the beam and sat there uneasily, their bodies tense, their hands resting nervously in their laps, ready to grab the steel beam in a dangerous gamble to save their lives. They noticed every slight vibration of the wooden bleachers through the rubber soles of their sneakers and through the corduroy of the seat of their pants. They were so alert to every creak and groan of the wooden planks that they paid no mind to Deputy Dogue as he took the podium and began lecturing on the virtues of looking both ways before crossing the street. Peter and Stan edgily waited as the speech droned on, but nothing happened. They scanned the crowd to see if they could detect an apparent sag in the bleachers anywhere, but everything was maddeningly normal. The assembly wore on the same way that assemblies always wore on, kids shifted uncomfortably as the wooden seats grew hard under their bottoms, and the teachers swiveled their heads to make sure Deputy Dogue was uninterrupted.

"Nothing is going to happen," Stan whispered sullenly. "Mr. Wisdom is just a crazy old nutcase."

"Be quiet, man, don't tempt fate."

"He's just a lunatic, man, a loony little…"

They both felt it simultaneously. A sharp, hard jolt through the strap metal they leaned their backs against. Then another, and another. Peter and Stan, in frantic unison, jumped up from their seats and grabbed the bottom lip of the I-beam, their fingers grasping for a firm grip in the greasy dust that covered the top of the rafter. They both squeezed their eyes shut as they swung from the ceiling, and they waited for the rush of air to blow past them as the bleachers collapsed. They waited for the anguished screams of hundreds of children to rise up to them, but everything was silent. Then they heard the first sounds. It was not the hideous shrieks of the maimed, but a titter, chuckling, and then full-blown laughter.

Peter slowly opened his eyes to see the bleachers still standing and every face in the crowd staring up at him as he dangled beside Stan. Uproarious cackling filled the immensity of the gymnasium, and Mrs. Whybrew furiously scaled the bleachers toward them.

"And that, boys and girls, is a perfect example of what not to do," Deputy Dogue boomed through the loudspeaker.

Peter let go of the girder and dropped back to bleachers. As he waited for Mrs. Whybrew to arrive, he looked over to where he and Stan usually sat, and he saw two fifth-grade boys laughing and rocking forward and then back against the strap metal that served as a backrest and barrier at the top of the bleachers. Peter slowly put his hand on the strap metal and felt the jolts as the fifth-graders rocked into it. Stan reached down and felt it too.

"I know a fifth-grader who's going to have problems after school today," Stan hissed.

Mrs. Whybrew hustled them down to the front row and sat them at the end, directly below their usual seats, and then she resumed her post at the center of the bleachers. Peter and Stan miserably waited for the laughter to subside and for Deputy Dogue to continue with his address. Mr. Wisdom's prediction now seemed ridiculous and sad, Peter thought. The fact that Mr. Wisdom said there was going to be an assembly today was just a coincidence. Mr. Wisdom was just a lonely outcast who tried to help in his own pathetic way.

"I'm going to the usual," Stan whispered as he ducked and slid between the bleachers and the wall," are you coming?"

"No, go ahead. I'm in enough trouble for one day."

Peter sat there alone and wondered what Mrs. Whybrew would do when assembly was over. Would he and Stan get kicked off of safety patrol? Would Mr. Patterson call his mother in? Peter wished that he had never heard of Mr. Wisdom. Peter sat and mulled over his predicament, still faintly feeling the bump of the fifth-grader rocking against the strap metal of the bleacher top when he heard a bewildered squeal and then a strange, splintery thump from behind the bleachers. Mrs. Whybrew scrambled to the top of the bleachers where the fifth-grader had now burst into panicked sobs, and Peter ducked between the bleachers and the wall, trying to see Stan in the gloom of the steel mazework, a sick feeling knotting his stomach.

As Peter fought his way through the tangle of girders and struts, he could see Stan sitting motionlessly, his back against the cool concrete block wall. When Peter finally clambered to Stan's side he stopped in horror. Stan, though unhurt, was ghostly pale, and his finger shook as he slowly pointed up to where Mrs. Whybrew peered over the back of the bleachers, the fifth-grader clinging to her waist. Peter could see, clearly in the light at the top of the bleachers, the place where the strap metal had given way at the welds from the repeated pounding from the fifth-grade boy's back. An eight-foot piece was missing from the back of the bleachers, and Peter, slowly looking back down beside his terrified friend, saw that the weld had broken as cleanly as an arrow point, and that its weight, from falling that distance, had driven the metal spear inches into the hardwood floor. The strap metal stood by itself, quivering in the boards of the gym floor, only a foot from where Stan sat shivering, but dead center in Peter's usual place.

The next morning snow was falling in big, cottony flakes at seven forty-five when Mr. Wisdom appeared at the alley mouth and shuffled across the street.

Peter eagerly stepped into the middle of the crosswalk and vigorously waved at the old man, but Mr. Wisdom, his head down against the snow, either didn't see Peter or, if he did, didn't acknowledge his presence. Mr. Wisdom carefully sat his paper bag down at the foot of the fence, and, as Peter stared incredulously, Mr. Wisdom took off his trench coat and gingerly bundled it around his sack. Mr. Wisdom then pressed his face against the icy chain link and gripped the fence with the red claws of his gnarled hands. He shivered violently, and Peter could hear the steady muffled rattle of the chain link against the steel posts through the heavily-falling snow.

Peter paced to the center of the crosswalk and then back to the opposite curb. And then Peter paced into the middle of the crosswalk again. What in the world is he doing, Peter wondered in exasperation. Peter paced back to the opposite curb and peeled off his gloves, stuffing them into the pockets of his coat, and then fumbled to open the buttons of the snow-flap on his parka. As he glanced down to grope with the last button, Peter heard the rattling of the chain link cease, and he looked back up to see Mr. Wisdom sit down hard on the snowy sidewalk. Before Peter could look both ways up and down the empty street, Mr. Wisdom had scrabbled to his feet and clutched the coat-wrapped bag to his chest and staggered off the curb. Mr. Wisdom lurched and reeled across the wintry street, and, as he tried to step up onto the opposite curb, he fell in a raggedy heap.

Peter flew to where the old man had fallen, shucking off his parka so that it trailed from his wrists in the air and thick snow. The old man had fallen on his side, with his head resting on the paper bag, and Peter knelt beside him and covered him with the parka. The old man was so small that Peter noticed his coat covered him entirely, like a blanket. As Peter tried to tuck the coat around Mr. Wisdom, the old man struggled and then lay still.

"Don't fight me, Mr. Wisdom," Peter pleaded. "Keep this on you, and I'll go get help."

Mr. Wisdom said nothing and closed his eyes. Peter could see the old man's breath rise in short, ragged gasps in the frosty air. Snowflakes fell and gathered on his bushy eyebrows. Peter clambered to his feet in the accumulating snow and began to run toward the school. Molly's post was the closest to his own, but he would have to scale three fences. Instead, Peter ran the long way toward Stan's post at the front gate, yelling at the top of his lungs.

"Emergency! Emergency!" Peter screamed as he rounded the last corner at the front entrance of the school. Children stopped their playing to watch him. Finally, Peter saw Stan at the front steps, sweeping away the snow from the walk with a broom. Peter stopped at the gate, panting plumes of vapor into the air.

"Stan," Peter called, "have someone call an ambulance. Mr. Wisdom collapsed back by my post. I think he's in bad shape."

Without replying, Stan dashed inside. Peter turned and began running back to where he had left Mr. Wisdom on the empty street. As Peter ran, he could see the children on the playground running toward the back of the school. Because he had to run around the fenced playground, a large crowd of children had already gathered at the back fence when he turned the last corner and sprinted to the old man lying in the gutter.

"It's okay, Mr. Wisdom," Peter panted, "an ambulance is on its way right now. You just hang on for a little more."

Peter, from where he knelt beside the old man, reached down and held the parka close around the old man's neck. Mr. Wisdom's breathing had become irregular. The vapor from his exhalations came in two or three short puffs followed by a long, thin stream that rose among the snowflakes. Then, there would be no cloud at all, and, just when Peter thought that the old man had stopped breathing, a few short puffs would appear again. Peter didn't know what to do but hold the parka close around the old man, and, thankfully, Peter heard, muffled and distant, the wail of a siren.

"They're on their way, Mr. Wisdom. You hold on. They're coming right now," Peter sobbed as he held the frail figure.

The siren grew louder and was joined by a second one coming from the opposite direction. Finally, an ambulance fish-tailed around a corner several blocks down and sped toward them, the flashing lights reflecting off the windows of the houses in the dim morning. In the other direction down the street, a police car shrieked toward them.

As the emergency medical crew raced from their vehicle and hunkered beside Mr. Wisdom with their equipment and instruments, Peter stood up and backed away from the old man.

"What happened, kid?" the ambulance driver asked Peter.

"He just fell down," Peter replied, his lower lip trembling, "he stands at the fence every morning…"

"He just fell down? Has he had any seizures? Has he been jerking around?"

"No. He seems to be having trouble breathing. I just held my coat around…"

"Do you know who he is?"

"His name is Mr. Wisdom."

"Does he live around here?"

"I don't know. I see him here every day…"

"Do you know if he has any relatives?"

"No. I mean I don't know if he does."

"Okay. Thanks, kid. You did a good job."

The emergency crew rolled Mr. Wisdom onto a children's stretcher and loaded him into the back of the ambulance. An oxygen mask was taped to his face, and another crew member began inserting an I.V. as Mr. Wisdom lay in the back of the van. The driver closed one of the pair of back doors and reached for the other one when Peter cried out.

"Wait," Peter called as he retrieved the paper bag with the trench coat wrapped around it, "this is his. I don't think he'd want to leave it here."

Peter rushed to the open door and pressed the sack into a space by Mr. Wisdom's head. The driver slammed the door shut and ran around to the front, slid in, and whisked the ambulance down the street in the snow, lights flashing and siren moaning. The police car followed, and the officer waved at Peter as he drove by. It was Deputy Dogue.

Peter watched the vehicles until they turned out of sight, and then he looked across the street, toward the school. There, while Mr. Wisdom had been unconscious, oblivious to the world, strapped to the gurney, had stood a hundred children, their faces pressed to the cold chain link, silent and watching.

Peter suddenly realized that the paramedics had taken his parka with Mr.

Wisdom. Peter looked down at his watch. It was eight twenty. As the children slowly scattered from their watch at the fence, Peter began walking to the janitor's room, cold and off-schedule.

The next day, Peter had no hope that Mr. Wisdom would emerge from the alley at seven forty-five, but, when Mr. Wisdom really did not show up, Peter was strangely disappointed. The snow had stopped the night before, and today was clear and bright with the sun reflecting off three inches of snow. Peter and his mother had listened to the radio since five that morning, waiting to see if a snow day had been declared, but school was open as usual. Most of the parents must have taken the snow day for granted, as had more than a few teachers, because attendance was minimal. The few students who did show up were being kept inside in the gymnasium before school so that the single yard-duty teacher who had arrived could keep a better eye on them. No one had come by Peter's post all morning.

Again, for some reason Peter could not fathom, he found himself walking across the street to the corner where Mr. Wisdom had kept his watch all autumn and into winter. Peter raised up his hands and clutched the chain link and pressed his face to the fence so that he could see clearly through one diamond in the pattern. The snow blanketing the playground was perfect, new, unsullied by any footprints. The field was like a promise before that promise has been thrown into the world, and because of the world, broken. The field, with its flawless covering of white, was an ideal. Later, Peter knew, the snow would melt, and he would be able to see the places where the grass was worn down to bare dirt, and the discarded wrappers from candy bars would be blown against the fences. But now the field was perfect. It was full of hope and promise.

"Get out of my place," Mr. Wisdom growled.

Peter whirled around. Mr. Wisdom stood before him, a brutal scowl darkening his face.

"Get out of my place."

"Mr. Wisdom! Are you feeling better? I didn't expect to see you..."

"Get out of my place."

Peter was rooted to the ground, paralyzed with fear. Mr. Wisdom took a short, odd-gaited step toward Peter and shifted the paper bag up closer to his chest.

"Leave. Now."

Peter could not move. His breath came high and hard in his throat. He could feel his heart knock the inside of his ribs.

"Leave now. This is yours."

Mr. Wisdom thrust his hand into the paper bag, stuffing his whole arm to the bottom. Then slowly, as he pulled an object through the scraps of rags and spine-broken books, Peter could see his arm emerge from the sack. Peter watched, frozen to the spot, like a deer in a car's headlights, until he saw Mr. Wisdom's hand rise above the edge of the paper bag, and, clenched in the dwarf's deformed claw, was a handful of hair.

Peter tore himself from the fence and ran across the street, not looking back for fear of what he might see. Peter slipped on the icy street and slid into the curb, crawling on all fours to get the street between himself and Mr. Wisdom. As he scrambled up the slick sidewalk, he saw, out of the corner of his eye, a big refrigeration truck come bouncing out of the alley at a good clip, and as the driver tried to turn onto the street, the tires lost traction on the icy road and the truck began spinning out of control. Slowly, as if in a dream, the huge truck revolved crazily across the street and jumped the curb at the corner, going backward, sheared off the fire hydrant and ripped the chain link fence from the ground. The truck finally came to a rest with its tandem rear wheels resting on Mr. Wisdom's spot.

Peter, with sickening dread, ran back across the street as the driver kicked open his door and crawled down from the cab. A fence post had punctured the truck's radiator, and steam and a torrent of water from the broken hydrant enveloped the corner in a thick cloud. The driver saw Peter dodging in and out of the periphery of the cloud, calling out a name.

"Whoa, son. Get out of there," the driver said as he grabbed Peter from behind and pulled him from under the rear of the truck.

"Mr. Wisdom!" Peter shouted as he twisted in the driver's grasp.

"Get out of here," the driver snarled.

"You ran over him! You hit him with your truck," Peter sobbed.

"Get out of here before I..." The driver hesitated when he saw a police car pull up across the street.

"What's going on here?" Deputy Dogue said gruffly.

"He ran over him," Peter yelled as he broke free from the driver and crawled toward the rear of the truck, feeling his way through the steam cloud and stinging spray of water.

"Who?" the deputy called after Peter.

"Mr. Wisdom!"

Deputy Dogue got on his hands and knees and crawled into the steam cloud also. With his baton, he poked into the mist until he felt a body. As Peter yelled from under the truck, the deputy reached in and pulled a person from between the wheels. It was Peter.

"Deputy, let me go..." Peter whimpered as he struggled to break free.

The deputy held Peter in his lap, and the radiator finally emptied itself. The cloud dissipated, and Peter frantically looked under the rear tires. All Peter could see was a soggy lumped pinned beneath the gigantic tires.

"Take it easy, boy," Deputy Dogue whispered to Peter. "It's okay. It's okay."

Exhausted, Peter gave up his struggling, and the deputy held him, holding Peter's head with his wet hand to keep Peter from looking under the truck.

"You did all you could about Mr. Wisdom," the deputy said softly, "so don't take it so hard."

"Help him, please, help him."

"Son, calm down. We can't help him now, it's too late. But I can tell you that the old man went easy. He didn't have any pain. He just closed his eyes and went away."

Peter gave the deputy a puzzled look.

"I was there. I saw it all. The emergency crew couldn't revive him at the hospital yesterday. When they took the oxygen mask off him, and he lay there, perfectly still, gone from this world, he had the biggest smile on his face. He went easy."

"No," Peter cried as he wrested himself from the deputy's grasp. The officer, bewildered, loosened his grip, and Peter crawled to the tires where he saw, now, that there was no body crushed beneath the truck. There, resting against one tire, was a sopping, greasy paper bag. Spilling from the top was wet, matted fur. Peter, with one trembling, outstretched hand, grasped the bag and pulled it toward him. It disintegrated at his touch, and, laying there in the soaked tangle of scraps of rags and spine-broken books, was no head, but Peter's missing parka.

The Insomniac

Percy slowly opened his eyes and blinked them, his eyelids gritty from lack of sleep. He was standing in a living room, in front of a grandfather clock, and the clock began to chime one o' clock. Percy felt a wave of confusion and panic sweep over him, as if he were being slowly immersed in a deep pool of cool water. Percy looked around the dark room, and it seemed both familiar and strange. Percy assumed that he had been sleepwalking again and had just awakened here in this living room, in front of this grandfather clock, but he could not remember going to sleep. The car accident had been weeks ago. Months, maybe? It was the night of the accident that these episodes had begun, the blurring of waking and sleeping. Consciousness was no longer the sunny procession of hours and days briefly interrupted by the dark flight of dreams and sleep. His recognition of the world, his perception and awareness of it, was a floating observation of dim images where time did not flow from one experience to another but jerked and spasmed. In fact, the only event in Percy's memory was his standing in this shadowy room at one o' clock. The rest of his memory was a wavering, black wall. When had he been here last? Last night? Last week? Percy, for the life of him, did not know.

Percy walked to the overstuffed green couch that sat before the fireplace and placed his hand on the back of it, gently squeezing the cool, slick fabric. Percy stared into the darkness of the hearth and struggled to remember something, anything, about this room. He turned and meticulously scanned the contents of the living room. The grandfather clock, the tall, dark oak china cabinet, the wide bookcase that loomed to the ceiling, the low, battered end tables, the elegant French doors with their puffy, sheer curtains. Moonlight slanted in through them onto the sturdy coffee table. A book lay open on the table. Percy picked it up, a large, hard-covered book about quilts. Percy turned a few of the glossy pages, vacantly noticing the photographs of quilts in different patterns, and then he sat it down. Quilts? Percy had never had any interest in sewing or quilts.

Percy turned back toward the fireplace with its massive oak mantle and studied the brick wall above it. Framed photographs had been hung helter-skelter around an immense oil painting which was centered over the hearth. Percy glided around the couch and scrutinized the photographs. Now he could see that the arrangement of the frames was due to the brick wall itself. Nails protruded from wherever the picture-hanger had found a crack in the mortar between the bricks to drive them in. One clot of photos followed a stair-stepping crack which ran to the left of the oil painting. Percy peered at the photographs, most of them old black-and-white Polaroids. In several of them, a young woman was frolicking at a beach. Most of these pictures showed her at a distance, running from the cresting surf or posing coyly on a blanket flung on the foot-print-pocked sand. But one of them was of her face. In it, she was gazing away from the camera, in a semi-profile that complimented her long, delicate nose and her dainty chin. Her eyes were large and wide-set, pretty in a homely sort of way. Her face radiated an attractive glow, although Percy could not tell whether this was because of the way the moonlight reflected off the glass covering the old photo or because the background of the picture was washed out by the old sunlight reflecting off the old sea. Percy had no idea who this woman was.

Percy turned his attention to the formidable oil painting hanging in the center of the photographs, like a blimp surrounded by a flock of gulls. This painting was also of a woman, but a different woman. The painting was done in an old style where the subject was costumed as a fox hunter, replete with red jacket and jodhpurs, tall, black riding boots and white cravat, and the ridiculous black cap. This woman stared uncomfortably from the painting, and even the wide-hipped riding outfit could not disguise the overwhelming truth that she was short and squat. Her blonde hair was severely swept back into a bun, Percy supposed, that was hidden under her cap. She did not smile so much as grimace, and, perhaps because her face was so wide and dowdy, the tip of her nose was close enough to the little, round ball of her chin to suggest that she were toothless. At her feet, instead of a pack of beagles, was a white gaggle of Pomeranians. Suddenly, from the depths of the dark water of Percy's memory, there rose the name, Mrs. Harpool. Mrs. Harpool! She was Percy's landlady. Miraculously, a vision of her, swathed in a tenty dress, struggling up the path through the rose garden as she grasped a handful of leashes and gummed curses at the Pomeranian mob that jostled before her, flooded Percy's mind. He rented this place from her. This was Percy's apartment. But why the quilt book? The end tables were crowded with figurines and music boxes sitting on lacy doilies. Percy picked up these knickknacks, one at a time, and turned them over in his hand, trying to decipher their meaning. Then he replaced them on the tables, trying to arrange them back in the order in which he found them, but failing. These things were never his. And the photographs! Who was this woman? Percy shuddered as a thought occurred to him. Did he have another life that occupied the dark times that hovered, out of reach, of his present memory. Had he married, he thought in horror, and not even realized it?

A small noise from upstairs roused Percy from his agitating thoughts. Or was it a noise? Wringing his hands, Percy began to question everything around him. It had been a noise, he assured himself. It had sounded like a bed creaking, or bare feet padding along a wooden floor maybe. Percy went to the bottom of the staircase but saw no light from the hallway at the top of the stairs. Carefully, he rose up the stairs and stood at the end of the hallway, listening for the sound of someone there. Nothing but silence. Percy went through the doorway into the bedroom and noticed that the bed was unmade, rumpled, as if someone had just risen out of it, the sheet and blanket thrown back to the foot of the bed. Had he been sleeping here before he awoke to find himself downstairs before the clock? He didn't know. Percy didn't know if he had even been sleeping before he found himself in the living room, let alone where. Everything was so disjointed. Percy went to the bed and sat on the edge of the mattress. The color of the sheets, barely discernible in the darkness, was pink. The sheet also had a tiny, floral print. Percy had never owned sheets like these. He raised the covers to his face and held them under his nose. He could smell the faint ghost of perfume. If he had married, where was his wife? Who slept in this bed, and where were they? Percy, even though he was exhausted, stood up, enervated by the mystery.

Percy walked across the room to the closet and slid open the mirrored door. Again, he was aware of the faint aroma of perfume. He pondered the garments hanging inside, all dresses. There were no men's clothes at all. He bent down and examined the shoes laying on the closet's floor, all heels and pumps. No men's shoes. Percy raised his arms to rummage through the shelf above the clothes rack, and, in his nervousness, toppled an empty hat box. As he quickly stooped and replaced it on the shelf, Percy heard a sustained, throaty growl. Percy whirled to see, slowly emerging from around the foot of the bed, the long head of a dachshund. The dog sluggishly ambled into full view, his fangs bared, his hackles straight up. Percy cautiously took a step toward the door, anxiously waiting for the dog's response. The dachshund, his legs bowed, his long belly dragging the ground, only continued to growl at the spot where Percy had been, seemingly unaware that Percy had moved. Percy, slowly and evenly, exhaled his held breath and retreated out of the door, thankful for the old dog's failing sight.

Percy very gently descended the stairs, but, halfway down, he grabbed the railing and slumped against it to keep from falling. The thought that occurred to him had made him weak in the knees. Amnesia! he thought. Maybe he was suffering from amnesia, and, slowly, by bits and pieces, he was remembering his old life. Maybe he lived somewhere else now, as a different person, but his recollection of his life before the accident had caused him to wander back, to reclaim the life that had been jarred from his head in the crash. The idea thrilled him and sickened him at the same time. Although the notion would explain the lapses of memory and the strange familiarity of this place, it also meant that now, as he lurked on the dark stairs, he was a trespasser. Percy held his breath and listened more intently than he ever had before. Was that water coursing through the plumbing buried deep in the walls? Were those bare footsteps whisking down the wooden hallway? Percy listened harder, and harder, but he heard nothing, absolutely nothing.

Frantic, Percy found himself at the French windows, and he passed through them into the rose garden. The night was cool. It must have been early summer because every rose bush held a dozen blooms. In the waning moonlight, Percy went to his favorite place in the garden, to the bench at the center of the concentric walks, and he sat down, exhausted but wide-awake. Percy buried his face in his hands and agonized over his thoughts. If I am recovering from amnesia, he thought, then who have I been since the accident? Where do I live? Are there people who will be worried about me? Where are my things? Percy threw back his head and wanted to cry, but then he became aware of the tranquility of the rose garden around him. As it often had before, the garden calmed Percy and cleared his head. Percy rose in the perfectly still air, in that darkest hour before dawn, and strolled through the garden, pulling the newly bloomed roses to his face and breathing in their delicate fragrances. The perfume of the roses gave him peace, as it had always done before, and Percy no longer worried about who or where he was. He walked the entirety of the garden, pulling the tall blossoms down to breathe in their fragile, exquisite scent, and he resolved to ask the first person he saw to help him find out the answers to his questions, and not worry about those questions until then.

In the first glimmer of dawn, Percy looked up at his apartment, and, through the French windows, saw a middle-aged woman dressed in her robe and nightgown standing at the end tables gazing curiously down at the figurines and music boxes. Percy recognized her from the photographs, but she was much older now, her delicate chin doubled, her thin hair up in a tangle of curlers. She bent over the curios and arranged them back to their original order. The dachshund absently nuzzled her worn slipper. Percy rose up through the garden, ascended the steps to the French doors and passed through. The woman turned toward him, startled, and her wide-set eyes dilated to the size of saucers. Percy opened his mouth to try to calm her, but, instead of words, he heard a chilling, low moan reverberate through the small room. The woman screamed and dashed through the room to the kitchen, the dachshund following with its tail between its legs, yelping furiously. Percy, overcome with panic, ran to the heavy, oak front door, but, instead of opening it, Percy began to pass through it. He could feel the indescribable tickle of his molecules mingling with those of the wooden door, the infinitesimal friction between himself and the striated oak panel as he passed through it into still morning air, and then everything went black again.

The commotion drew the attention of a small girl who lived across the garden and who had wakened early, because she was worried about her favorite doll, and had witnessed the odd mystery of the roses bending, one by one, in the breathless air.

Daffodils

The air brakes screeched as the bus swung into its greasy berth at the station. Jenny lifted her head from the overstuffed bookpack she had been using for a pillow and peered into the dimness under the corrugated metal canopy where people milled and scuffled with baggage. She sat up and straightened her denim jacket, rubbed her cheek with the back of her hand and felt the imprint of the pack's zipper running from her high cheekbone to the corner of her mouth, like a freshly stitched scar. She kept her seat while the rest of the passengers grabbed their luggage from overhead and jostled each other down the aisle and out into the humid evening. When the bus had cleared, Jenny gathered her pack and the small suitcase she had crammed beneath the seat in front of her, glanced out of the window, and there, through her own pale reflection in the glass, she saw her grandfather hustle out of the terminal, fish a cigarette from his shirt pocket and light it as he inspected the crowd filing inside. When she descended the steps onto the sidewalk, he was waiting for her, the cigarette hanging from one corner of his crooked smile.

"There's my princess," he chortled.

He reached down and snatched the suitcase and bookpack with one hand, and with the other he crushed her to himself, his pack of smokes and lighter pressing into her temple. He smelled like he always did, of stale smoke and cheap aftershave lotion, a strangely pleasant sweaty aroma. He was hugging her the way he had always hugged her, since she could remember him stooping to enfold her in both big arms, but now, instead of being comforted by the familiarity of his embrace, she unexpectedly thought of how much she would miss him if she were never to see him again, and she began to sob.

"What's the matter, little princess," he said as he let the cigarette fall from his lips to the concrete where he ground it out with the toe of his boot. He knelt on one knee before her and looked up into her tear-stained eyes.

Jenny could not speak. The sobbing had diminished, but the back of her throat was still constricted and ached with her effort to stop crying. Anyway, he knew! she thought. Why was he going to make her say it, here, in public, in front of all of these strange people? She was ashamed of her outburst, but even more ashamed to give voice to the lousy truth that her parents had divorced, had each decided to take what was theirs and move on, turning their backs on her entire world. Her anguish was slowly displaced by frustration, and she sniffed loudly and fiercely dried her eyes with the back of her fist.

Her grandfather picked up her suitcase and pack in one hand and rested the other on her shoulder as they walked through the noise and bustle of the bus station. Although she knew that she was one small, insignificant part of the hum and tumult of the busy station, Jenny felt as if she floated apart from the crowd, barely gliding over the brilliant linoleum in the frigidly conditioned air. Her life, surely, was painfully unique, she thought; she must be special in her suffering, and kind. She shrugged her shoulders so that her grandfather's hand slipped down, and she took it in her own and led him out the front door.

Her grandfather swung her bags through the open window into the back of his old Cadillac, and she slid into the front passenger seat, the vinyl still warm from the evening sun. He nosed into traffic, and Jenny let herself be immersed in the flow of trees and houses rushing past the open window. The drive was familiar in that Jenny made it one or two times a year, mostly for spring break and a few weeks in the summer, but it was familiar in a way that only visits to relatives can be. Jenny noticed the big differences in the landscape as they rolled to her grandfather's house, the new Dairy Queen beside the mall, the apartment complexes that had sprouted up out by the bypass. But it was the little differences that tugged at her. She discovered that the small brick house on the corner of Elm and Main had been painted white. The man with the horse farm beside the high school had cut down the huge oak tree in the exercise lot. The ice house by the railroad tracks had its door boarded over. Jenny had always enjoyed this small town, how it seemed to be the same, a place outside of time where she spent a few summer weeks each year, a place, like a faithful hound, that would always wait for her to return. When her mother had suggested Jenny come here to spend a while, Jenny had rejoiced in the suggestion. She had thought that a familiar place might comfort her, take the edge off her own life at home that was changing in ways she had never imagined.

Jenny glanced out of the Cadillac window and noticed that the drive-in on the edge of town, the one where she and her family and her grandfather would go to see monster movies on warm summer evenings, had tall weeds growing through the asphalt, speakers hung from their posts and dangled, and the screen had a crescent rip through the center of it. Through her new eyes, Jenny could see that everything changed.

They were out of town now, winding through the small hills to her grandfather's place in the country. The sun had just set, and, as they swooped from hilltop to hollow in the old Cadillac, the air would chill as it rushed through the window. Then, as they rose to the next hill's crest, the air would warm again, and clouds of insects tattered as the car barreled through. When her grandfather pulled down his long clay road to his house, and that squat, white farmhouse swung into view from behind the old maples, Jenny leaned forward and grasped the dashboard and smiled. This place had not changed. As she and her grandfather walked through the screened-in porch into the cluttered front room, she smelled the usual faint aroma of fried beef and sweet cigars. The poster of a boy on a bicycle, a safety poster she had drawn in fourth grade that had won first prize in the school competition, still hung, framed, on the wall above the piano. And, on the piano top, lined up like trophies, were seven novelty figurine ashtrays, her birthday presents to him for the last seven years. Her grandfather tossed her bags on the dusty couch, and she followed him into the spartan kitchen and then out into the small yard behind the house. He twisted on the spigot above the galvanized horse trough, and the plashy spatter of water caused Lady Belle, an old chestnut mare, to amble from behind the storage shed and stretch her long neck over the rusted wire fence, the blaze on her forehead astonishingly white in the deepening dusk. Her grandfather climbed the two steps back into the house, and, as the screen door slapped shut, he flipped on the kitchen light. Jenny walked from the trough where Lady Belle nuzzled her palm with her huge soft lips into the yellow square of light that slanted through the back door and lifted the drinking dipper from its nail by the faucet. Jenny filled it, raised the dipper to her lips, and slowly relished the cool water, its mossy, metallic tang of tin. For the first time in months, Jenny relaxed. That old feeling of warmth coursed through her, that palpable sensation of security, like when she used to sit by herself, upstairs in her room at home, on a rainy evening reading a good book, her parents downstairs, on the couch together, and she would pull herself around her, like a comfortable robe. The throbbing sizzle of cicadas wound up from the distant tree line behind the barn, now enveloped in darkness. Then the telephone jangled from the kitchen wall.

"Hey, honey," Jenny's grandfather said from inside the bright house, "oh yeah, she got here fine. We got in just a little while ago. We're stretching our legs. She's visiting with Lady Belle out back. I'll get her."

But when he opened the back door to call his granddaughter, he only saw the tin dipper dully gleaming on the dark grass and heard the brittle, rhythmic crunch of footsteps running through the maple woods beside the house. He stooped to pick up the dipper and went back inside.

Her grandfather was setting the silverware beside the chipped blue plates when Jenny hesitantly opened the screen door and slipped into the kitchen. Foxtails pricked her ankles through her socks from where she had run into the brushy woods and had stopped and leaned against the maple bark to see her grandfather step back into the house after he called her. She had watched him, as he had crossed back and forth before the curtainless window of the back room, put fresh sheets on the bed she would be sleeping in, and, when the hungry scent of frying hamburger wafted to her, she had come back. Now, she sat in a kitchen chair and picked the burrs from her socks as her grandfather scooped the patties onto a paper towel-covered plate and pressed them with the spatula.

"One or two, to start with?" he asked as he carried the plate to the table.

"Grandpa," Jenny began, "I'm sorry..." but her throat tightened and she could feel the hot tears beginning to well.

"Stop that, princess. I told your mom that you had gone for a little walk. That's all. Now how hungry are you?"

Jenny looked up at her grandfather. An old, frilly apron incongruously protected his worn work clothes. A sound escaped from the back of her throat, half-sob, half-laugh.

"I mean it now. Any more crying out of you and you'll be sharing oats with Lady Belle out in the barn."

The softness in her grandfather's eyes betrayed his gruff tone, and Jenny quickly wiped her face with the paper napkin that had been folded neatly beneath her silverware.

"Two, Grandpa. And Lady Belle better watch out because I could eat a horse about now."

Her grandfather guffawed and forked two patties onto her plate. Jenny helped herself to heaping portions of hominy and field peas, and the two ate silently, the only sounds in the kitchen the voracious clatter of forks on the chipped blue plates, the hollow tock of the clock above the stove, and the insistent ebb and flow of the cicadas outside. When they were finished, Jenny cleared the table as her grandfather scraped his chair back to retrieve a cigar from the box on the sideboard. As he began his puffing ritual to light the cigar, Jenny returned to her chair, her belly full, and gazed around the starkly lit kitchen. Although her grandfather lived by himself, his kitchen was quaintly feminine. Lining the counter top by the sink was a set of crockery hand-painted with a flower design. The curtain over the window above the sink was also flowered. A spray of dusty plastic flowers sprouted from a white vase in the center of the table, an ornate doily under it. The old chrome toaster was protected by a crocheted cover, as was the electric coffeepot. The covers were made to look like dolls: the body sat up on the appliance while the doll's long skirt formed the actual cover. Sitting beside each other, the toaster and the coffeepot, they looked like Fat and Skinny, just before their race up the pillowcase. The kitchen made it seem like an old woman should be heard somewhere else in the house, humming while she dusted the bric-a-brac on the top of the piano. But that woman was many years gone, and Jenny turned her attention to that woman's photograph, where it hung on the wall over the stove beside the sonorous clock.

Her grandfather's wife, her mother's mother, her grandmother, had died before Jenny was born. She had died when Jenny's mother was still a girl. She had died so long ago that she was rarely mentioned anymore, not because she wasn't loved, but because the years had accumulated, each one with its own weight of dull, daily details, and life had gradually changed. In her absence, the usual rituals of maintaining a small farm had gone on, day after day, and Jenny's mother had married and left home, and the old ramshackle barn had been replaced with a gleaming galvanized one, and her grandfather's wife was simply no longer a part of the insistent world that greeted her grandfather every morning when he opened his eyes. Jenny gazed harder at the photograph above the stove, although she had seen it so many times that it had lost its meaning, like a word does when it is repeated over and over. The photograph showed a young woman standing beside an old pickup truck, wind blowing her long skirt and her long hair. Her grandfather had told her that the picture was taken after they had married and had moved to this place. But now, Jenny noticed something about the framed picture that she never had before. Not really the photograph itself, but the glass covering it and the ornate frame. Beside the picture, the clock, a white plastic circle with a circular pendulum swinging from it, the gold-toned paint covering it tarnished to a motley gray, had a greasy dust clinging to the stem of the pendulum. Tiny cobwebs, stained black by the smoke of thousands of hamburgers, joined the top of the clock to the yellow wall. But the photograph, with its lacy metal frame, was spotless.

"Do you still love Grandma?" Jenny blurted, immediately feeling a warm blush rise into her cheeks.

"Well, well, well," her grandfather clucked as he leaned forward to tap the ash off his cigar into a cracked saucer, "that's a heck of a question."

"I mean, do you still think about her, even though she's not here anymore?"

"Of course I think about her, Jenny," her grandfather said slowly, "and I still love her very much, even though she is gone."

"But how can that happen, when the people you love go away? How can you still love them when you know that they would rather be somewhere else, away from you?"

"Jenny, princess, you..."

"Never mind," Jenny interrupted, her voice rising, her throat constricting, "this isn't the same. I don't know why I asked you that. Grandma isn't here because she died. She couldn't help that. She didn't leave because she wanted to..."

"Jenny..."

"Maybe that's better, when people die. Maybe it doesn't hurt so bad when you know there was nothing you could do to stop them from leaving. Maybe if everyone in my family just died, I wouldn't feel so bad.."

Jenny threw herself from her chair, the sobs heaving up from her chest like fist-sized, smooth stones. She stumbled toward the screen door, but her grandfather was already there, his arms open, kneeling, and Jenny let herself fall into his embrace.

"Shh, princess, shh," her grandfather soothed as he scooped her up and carried her through the screen door, out into the dark yard. He sat down on the steps and held her in his lap, one large, calloused hand smoothing the hair away from her temples.

"Why don't they want me anymore?" Jenny whimpered with the sharp intake of breath between wails.

"Shh, baby, shh, baby," her grandfather cooed as he rocked her, "nobody doesn't want you anymore."

"But, they left..."

"Jenny, princess, just because your mom and dad are splitting up doesn't mean that they don't love you anymore. Sometimes two people change, and, when they change, they find out that they can't be together anymore."

"It's not supposed to be that way. We're supposed to be a family..."

"And sometimes families move apart from each other, princess. I don't know that it's wrong so much as it's different. You'll still see both of them."

"But it won't be the same."

"Princess, you know how you asked me how I felt about your grandmother? You asked me if I still loved her even though she's gone? Well, in some ways, she didn't leave. In some ways, she's not gone."

"What do you mean, she's not gone."

"I mean that there are many things that still remind me of your grandmother, and when I see or hear or touch these things, I feel as if she were close to me again. Even now, this many years after she died, she still leaves me gifts."

"Gifts," Jenny asked, her sobs diminishing, "what kind of gifts?"

"Little things that were special to her and me. I'll find them now and again as I'm working, and they'll make me think of her."

"I don't understand, Grandpa. She leaves things? Is she a ghost? Do you see her?"

"Ha, ha," her grandfather chuckled, "I guess you could say that she is a ghost of sorts, only I don't think she knows it."

"I don't understand, Grandpa," Jenny mumbled as she swiped at her eyes with the back of her arm.

"I'm trying to tell you that even though you think your life is going to change for the worse, and that nobody loves you, you're going to find gifts too, gifts that will remind you of the time when your family was together and help you make it when things seem really bad."

Jenny was exhausted, and she let her head lay against her grandfather's shoulder. Instead of anger or sadness, she felt hollow, as if everything inside her had been carved out and displaced with warm helium. She felt as if she could float up out of her grandfather's arms and disappear into the warm country night.

"Would you like me to show you one of these gifts?" her grandfather said gently as he carried her back into the house.

"Okay, Grandpa," she murmured.

"In the morning, then," he whispered, and he carefully placed her on the newly-made bed. She was asleep before he could turn out the light.

When her grandfather gently shook her, it was still dark outside the window of the bedroom.

"C'mon, sleepyhead, you said that you wanted to see the gift."

Jenny rubbed her eyes. The gift? she thought. And then she remembered what her grandfather had told her the night before, but in fragments, as if she were remembering the odd drama of a dream.

"The sun will be up soon. Let's go while it's still dark so we can see her bring it."

"See her?" Jenny said, now fully awake, her eyes wide.

"C'mon," her grandfather said, "we can have breakfast when we get back."

Jenny followed her grandfather out the back door into the yard where it was a little lighter although the morning was still a deep gray. She followed him closely to keep from stumbling into anything, her denim jacket pulled tightly around her in the cool predawn. They squeezed through the tall wooden gate to the horse pen, and, as they rounded the shed, Lady Belle whickered a greeting.

"Good morning, old girl," her grandfather said as he ran his hand down the horse's silky neck, "do you want to come see it too?"

The horse followed them all the way to the back of the horse lot, where, just beyond the barbed wire fence, the woods loomed thick and dark. Jenny's grandfather spread the wire fence, and Jenny knew to carefully duck between the strands. Once through, she spread the fence, pushing down hard on one strand with her foot and lifting mightily on the one above it, and her grandfather slipped through.

"I'll bet you didn't know that the first house your grandmother and I had on this place wasn't that one," he said, thumbing the air over his shoulder, "we first built back in these woods, before we figured out what sections we were going to clear and where the county road was coming in."

Jenny and her grandfather picked their way down what was now a tractor path, two beaten-down trails running parallel into the dense woods.

"It wasn't much of a house. I built it myself out of lumber I cut down making this road here. It wasn't but two rooms. We used the big room for the kitchen and living room, and then it had a small bedroom off the back of it."

As they went deeper into the dim forest, Jenny's eyes grew accustomed to the gloom. The old path grew narrower, and the grass between the ruts sprouted waist-high.

"Anyway, it wasn't much of a house, barely more than a log cabin, but your grandmother loved it. During the day, while I was busy running the saw mill, she spruced that place up like it was a castle. She kept the inside of that little place scrubbed up, and she raked out a little yard around the house in the clearing."

The light was growing stronger now, and Jenny could see through the trees, maples and pines, as they walked deeper into the woods.

"She sewed curtains for the windows and crocheted a really pretty table cloth. She saved up her egg money and bought a rug for the big room, had flowers all over it. She had me put window boxes outside of every window and she planted wild flowers in them."

Jenny's grandfather stopped and took Jenny's hand. They left the over-grown path and walked directly into the woods, following a path that was merely the absence of trees. The sun had dawned now, and through the trees, Jenny could make out the brightness of a clearing ahead of them.

"She worked herself to frazzle making that old place pretty. It was our first place that we owned as husband and wife, and she loved it no matter what."

They stepped out of the woods into a small clearing. The sun was fully above the horizon now, and the colors of the clearing strengthened from grays to greens and yellows.

"This is where it was," her grandfather continued, looking in the center of the clearing, "there isn't anything left of the house at all now. We took it apart and used it to build part of the old shed up there by the new house. There isn't a scrap of wood left here now. You wouldn't even now there'd ever been a place here."

Jenny, too, now stared at the center of the clearing, sunlight dappling the ground through the canopy of leaves.

"Except for the gift," he said as he squeezed Jenny's hand.

There, in the center of the clearing where no structure stood at all, was a circle of daffodils, slowly opening their bright yellow petals in the stream of morning light.

One Last Battle

"Hitler had flooded all of the fields. The whole countryside was under eight feet of water. Reconnaissance came back and told us it was like flying over a mirror that stretched from the beachheads back in forty miles. They told us there were a few places that weren't under, but Hitler had covered them with sharpened poles. Said those places looked like a porcupine treading water. We were supposed to jump in there the next day."

Papa Cogan paused to cram the stem of his church warden's pipe between his teeth and thumb a matchbox from the bib of his overalls. Paul looked up from where he sat on the porch steps and watched Papa light the bowl with a quick series of shallow smacks. A garland of blue smoke wreathed the air above Papa's head, and he rested the long-stemmed pipe between his thumb and forefinger on his knee.

"If a man jumped in that water, with his pack, his emergency chute, his gun, them heavy jumping boots, he was one man Hitler wouldn't have to worry about, because he would drown before he could cut himself out of all that gear. Of course there were a lot of men who would've preferred the water to jumping into the Nazzy pickets. I can remember floating down through darkness and watching the tracers zipping up toward us. They were the prettiest red shafts of light. You could hear them popping rips in the silk canopy of your 'chute. I've seen soldiers hanging dead in their harnesses as they drifted down out of the night. Once they hit the ground, their 'chutes will fill up with wind, like sails, and drag them until they snagged in a fence row or a tree line. There would be a bunch of dead paratroopers rolled up there like so many tumbleweeds. Mike Hanrahan saved his butt one time by crawling up in the middle of a pile of those dead ones and playing possum while a Nazzy patrol walked by."

Papa raised the pipe up to his mouth and clenched it between his teeth as he fumbled for another match and relit it. Paul turned from Papa and looked out across the flat field behind the house and imagined parachutes billowing limply to the ground in the middle of the chatter of automatic gunfire.

Paul heard voices from the side yard and then a loud grunt. Porter, Papa's youngest son, poked his head from around the side of the house and glared up at the old man.

"Mama wants to know if you're planning on bringing them peas home for supper sometime tonight," Porter said loudly.

Papa closed his eyes and slowly drew on his pipe. Paul peered past Papa at Porter who had a deep shade of crimson rising up from his neck and flushing in his jowls. Porter was the same age as Paul's father, but he was single and still lived on the farm with Papa and his mother. Paul would often hide in the horse shed and spy through a knothole across the twenty acres that separated his family's spread from Papa's as Porter fed the hogs. Nearly every morning Porter would stalk out to the pen behind Papa's house and herd the hogs up to the trough with a broad fence-slat. Paul would see the board whip down on the wide backs of the squealing mob, and, a second later, hear the thudding spank of wood on hide. Paul would watch the waggle of Porter's head and then hear the curses carry across the open field. Paul had never seen this ritual up close, but he imagined Porter's face to be as florid when he raged at the pigs as it was now as he waited for his father to answer.

"Tell your Mama that I will be there directly, son," Papa finally replied.

At that moment, Paul's mother pushed open the back door with a bushel basket of peas and carried it to the edge of the porch where Porter fumed.

"There you go, Papa," she said and whisked back through the screen door into the kitchen.

"Shake a leg, old man," Porter hissed, "or you'll miss your supper."

Porter spun on his heel, ignoring the basket of peas, and haughtily strode straight-legged across the meadow toward the hog-pen.

"Here, Papa, I'll carry it over for you," Paul said as he scurried around the corner of the porch to the basket.

"Have a seat, boy. We're in no hurry to get over there," Papa said, waving Paul away from the peas, "Supper won't be ready for a long while yet."

Papa shifted in the seat of his chair by half-raising himself on the arms and then slowly settling himself back down. With both hands, he reached down and lifted his left leg just above the knee and then dropped it, his heel landing with a hollow thump on the porch boards. Paul, who had returned to his roost on the porch steps, irresistibly stared at the oddly-scuffed boot that was wedged on over the wooden foot.

"Supper time, Paul," his mother called from inside the kitchen, "Ask Papa if he'd like to stay and eat with us."

"No thank you, Ruth," Papa called back over his shoulder, "but I wouldn't mind sitting here a while longer and enjoying your beautiful sunset."

"Suit yourself, but I cooked up two fryers. We've got plenty to feed another hungry mouth."

"C'mon, Papa," Paul pleaded, offering his hand to help the old man out of the chair.

"Go on, boy. I'll wait for you to get finished before I leave."

Paul backed slowly through the screen door, watching the back of Papa's head as he rummaged through his bib pocket for his elusive matchbox.

Paul slapped through the screen door onto the porch, wiping chicken grease from the corners of his mouth, and tripped over Papa's cane which had been propped against his chair. The clatter roused Papa from a catnap, and the old man jerked his chin up from his chest, wide-eyed, and frantically groped the air around his chair for his cane, like a sentry caught without his rifle.

"Here, here, who goes there?" Papa barked down the porch steps.

"It's me, Papa," Paul whispered as he snatched up the fallen cane and handed it to the old man.

"Don't scare a man like that, son. An old timer like me might just keel over."

Papa sat up and replaced the cane beside him and retrieved his pipe which had fallen from his lap.

"Were you dreaming about the war, Papa?"

"I always dream about the war, boy. The damned thing won't let me go."

"Nightmares, Papa, like seeing dead people?"

"Naw, just faces, and things that happened. Just now I was dreaming about sitting in a vineyard outside a little French town, drinking wine."

"The town where you lost your foot?"

"Yeah, that was the place."

"Where Mike Hanrahan got killed?"

"Yeah, but, in the dream, he's still alive, and we're drinking wine together."

"Tell me about how he got killed, Papa. Tell me all of that story."

"Don't be a ghoul, boy. There's shouldn't be any pleasure in hearing about how a person got killed."

"Please, Papa. I want to know. I want to know what is was like."

"Let me tell you about..."

"Please, Papa. Tell me about that place. Tell me about you and Mike."

Papa, in the dwindling light, looked down at Paul on the steps, and, for the first time, maybe because the dream was still fresh, or maybe because Paul, Papa could tell, really wanted to know what happened, without judgment or question, Papa gave words to the story he had held nameless for fifty years. The hysteria and excitement of that time washed over him again.

"It was about two weeks after we got a foothold in France, and Mike and me, our squad, were rolling the Nazzies back toward Germany, fighting from town to town. One night we cleared out this little hamlet, this little-bitty town that wasn't but a church and school and a handful of houses. We had come up on it that afternoon. We'd covered over twenty miles that day, which was quite a ways because those Nazzies weren't giving up easy. Anyway, we were real surprised we got that far, and we were even more surprised when we saw the Nazzies clearing out of this little town as we came up the road toward them. They didn't fire a single shot. They just loaded up about a half dozen halftracks and skedaddled out the back door. We pulled up about a quarter mile from the village and sent pickets around either side. The pickets checked out the town, sneaking door to door, to see if there was anybody hanging around, you know, trying to lure us into a trap, but, sure enough, the whole lot of them had cleared out. In fact, all the people that lived there had cleared out too. The whole place was empty as a poor man's belly.

"Me and Mike went snooping around the old church because sometimes there would be people hiding down in the basement. Church basements were a favorite hiding spot for them Frenchmen. That wasn't too smart, because if I could figure that out in a couple of weeks, I'm sure them Nazzies had it figured out too. But, anyway, we crept down there, but the place was empty. Not a soul. What we did find, though, made us a whole lot happier than a bunch of old men and women and kids hunkering in the dark. We found the biggest wine cellar that I'd ever seen. We wondered why a church had this much booze stashed in the basement, and Mike, who was an Irishman and a good Catholic, said that it must all be sacramental wine. I told him that if a church had that much wine on hand then they must have Communion three times a day, all week long. We were real surprised, too, that the Nazzies hadn't tore the place up. They were real good about wrecking places before they left them. Sure, there were a couple dozen empty bottles laying around the floor, so we figured that a few soldiers had probably gone down and had a party, maybe figured on keeping what they found quiet so they'd have a nice stash if they hung around for very long. There must have been a thousand bottles down there, all lined up in these dusty old oak racks. Me and Mike each grabbed four bottles and headed out of there.

"On the other side of this little place was a vineyard. It had a little stone wall around it, just a few rocks piled on top of each other, really, and , inside, were rows and rows of grapevines tangled all over these wooden poles. We figured that maybe this vineyard was why there were so much wine at the church; maybe they bottled it there. Anyway, me and Mike crawled over the wall into that vineyard and sat back under some grapevines. That day had been hot, but now it was cooling off, especially in the shade there in the vineyard. Our patrol had sent pickets a mile down the road where the Nazzies had gone, to make sure they didn't sneak back up on us, and we could hear mortar fire off to the north of us, but a long way away, probably ten miles or so, so me and Mike relaxed there in the shade and started drinking that wine. That was the first time we'd been able to kick back and relax since we'd got to France.

"Anyhow, we sat there and drank that wine. The rest of the patrol had set up in the church, but me and Mike stayed out there in the vineyard as the sun set and the whole countryside got dark. After two weeks of hand-to-hand, it was real peaceful out there. We got to talking about how much we missed home. Mike's family, you know, owned this section that your pa owns now. We'd grown up together, and we'd joined up in the Army together, and, as we sat in that vineyard, it seemed real strange that two country boys that had never been twenty miles from home before the war started were sitting drinking wine in France, half the world away from everything that we knew. The stars came out, and the moon. It was real bright that night, and we ended up drinking all of that wine we brought out there with us.

"Now, neither one of us was much of a drinker. My daddy and Mike's daddy both were teetotalers. If they'd caught us drinking like that on the farm, we'd have got our hides tanned. But we were in France, and we figured we deserved a break. We thought we were men. We started boasting to each other about how brave we'd been, how we could lick our weight in Nazzies in our sleep. And then Mike started getting weepy on me. He started telling me how I was his very best friend in the whole world. He told me that, if it weren't for me being there with him, he would have tried to get out of the Army and come back home. He said that he was awful homesick, but, because we were there together, he'd be able to tough it out. He said all he could think about was getting back home, when this was all over. Then I made some dumb comment about whether or not we would ever get back home. Mike put his arm around me and looked me in the eyes, real serious, and he said, 'Buddy, don't you worry about that. I'll take care of you. I'll make sure that you get home okay. I'll make sure that a bullet don't send you home in a box.' And I told him that I'd do the same for him, and we sat there, leaned back up under those grapevines, bone-tired from two weeks of war, two friends in the middle of a foreign land, and we fell asleep.

"I don't know what woke me up the next morning, but, for some reason, I opened my eyes, and I saw, on the other side of the stone wall, walking up the road, a bunch of Nazzies. Somehow they had gotten past our pickets, killed all of them. Just moving my eyes, I glanced beside me and saw Mike still asleep under the grapevines. The Nazzy patrol on the other side of the wall stopped and circled up, leaning their helmets together and talking to each other, like they were deciding what to do next. What I didn't know at the time was that they had already found the rest of our patrol in the church. Our guys had found the wine too, and they were all sleeping off a drunk when the Nazzies burst in and killed them. Me and Mike must have got pretty drunk too, because we slept through all of that. I thought that the Nazzies hadn't seen me and Mike though, because we were up under the vines pretty good. And even though we had got drunk, we had the sense to keep our rifles near us. Mine was laying near my feet, in the grass, but out from under the grapevines, and Mike's was beside mine. We still had our clips and grenades on our belts though.

"Anyway, I sat there real still. I was hoping that the Nazzies would move on soon, and me and Mike could sneak down the row of vines and crawl into the next field and try to rendezvous with the rest of our guys. As I watched them stand in that circle and talk, I saw a rifle barrel rise up over the shoulder of a Nazzy whose back was to me. They knew we were there, and they were pretending to talk so they could get a shot off at us. A Nazzy on the far side of the circle was using his pals as a blind, and I realized that he was taking a bead right between my eyes. In the same instant that I realized that Nazzy was going to shoot me, I heard Mike holler from beside me and the rifle go off. I tried to jump forward and grab my rifle, but Mike threw himself in front of me, and I heard the bullet hit his helmet. I snatched up my rifle and started firing at them, and I hit one trying to come over the wall. The rest of them ducked down behind the stones and returned fire. I grabbed Mike and pulled him deep into the grapevines with me. I kept firing at the wall from inside the vines to keep their heads down, and then I pulled a grenade from my belt and lobbed it the twenty yards to the wall, and it bounced once and rolled up to the bottom of the wall on my side. I pushed us even deeper in the vines and rolled myself on top of Mike just as the grenade went off. It blew a big hole in the wall and killed a couple of the Nazzies and scattered the rest. I jumped up out of the vines and started picking off the rest of them as they wandered around in the road, dazed by the concussion of the blast.

"When I was sure there weren't any more of them on the other side of the wall, I knelt down to Mike, who was still just laying there, and pulled off his helmet to see where the bullet had got him, but he didn't have a mark on him. The bullet had ricocheted off his helmet, leaving a little dent in the metal right over the temple. It had walloped him good in the head and knocked him cold. Even though I was scared to death and my hands were shaking so hard I could barely hold my rifle, I started to giggle about the headache Mike would have when he woke up. A hangover and a whack in the head to boot. I shook him until he started to wake up, and then he started thrashing around there in the grapevines. I held him, and he opened his eyes, and they were real wide and glassy. I asked him if he was okay, but all he kept asking was whether Mom would be upset that we had been out all night. That bullet had knocked the sense clean out of him.

"I got him up on his feet and handed him his rifle, but he was awful confused and kept asking about his momma. He kept telling me that we were going to be in big trouble for staying out all night. I got us over the wall and back up into the town, and when we got to the church and went inside, I saw what had happened to rest of our patrol. When we came back out, I could hear heavy armor moving up the road to the town from the east. What I didn't know then was that the place where we had pushed so far ahead the day before had made a gap on either side of us, and the reason the Nazzies had cleared out so quick was to go get reinforcements to try to tear through this hole. What we heard coming down the road was half a Panzer division rumbling up to cut our line and flank the troops to the north. I took Mike by the hand, just like he was a little kid, and led him back through the town to the west, to try to get back to the unit that was behind us. Our troops, since they couldn't contact my patrol after they were killed that morning, had expected the worst and had poured in every available soldier into our breach, most of them green recruits. Just as we got to this big, open field west of town, Mike started getting upset and argued with me. He kept telling me that we were going the wrong direction to get home. He said that we had to go the other way, through the woods, to get back to the house. I was frantic. The Nazzy tanks were almost into town, and I didn't know whether to argue with him or just pick him up over my shoulder and carry him. I had my mind made up for me.

"Artillery, mortar fire started falling on the town thick and fast. The church came down in a thick cloud of dust and smoke. Another round hit between us and the church and blew us over. From out of the rubble of the town, the Panzers crashed through and opened up their turret cannons on the treeline on the other side of the field. I threw Mike over my shoulder and took off for that treeline at a dead run. Mike was my size, and heavy, and I let our rifles slip off my shoulder and fall in the weeds. I was running flat out as fast as I could. The treeline was a hundred and fifty yards away, and I wanted to put most of that distance behind me before the Nazzy infantry came up behind the tanks. As I got closer to the woods, I could see puffs of smoke rising through the trees off to my right where our artillery was firing on the town. By the time I got seventy-five yards from the trees, I could see our boys dug in, hiding behind the tree trunks. About that same time, I heard the rifle fire open up behind me, and I saw the grass twitching around me and heard the little thuds of bullets smacking the earth at my feet. When I got fifty yards from the treeline, a medic and a dozen of our boys started running into the field for us. Our soldiers were firing as they ran, putting down fire for cover. Just as the medic reached me, twenty-five yards from our line, I saw a fireball explode in the treeline, exactly in the place I was running to, and then another, in a line between the first explosion and me, and another and another, each closer, until I stumbled into the medic and flames climbed over us, and everything went black.

"When I came to, the grass I was laying in was smoldering, and the air was closed in with smoke. I could barely see the forest, but, in the places where the smoke thinned out, I could see dead men hanging in the trees. Mike was laying beside me, and I could tell from the look on his face that he was dead. When I tried to get up, I realized that my foot was gone. The wound was burned bad, so there wasn't any bleeding hardly. That's what probably saved my life. I sat back down and listened to see if I could tell what was going on, but everything was quiet. I started to think about what I'd told Mike, about keeping him safe, and, I'm not ashamed to tell you boy, I started crying like a little girl. I didn't seem like I could even hear myself cry, and I got worried that I'd gone deaf. But then, as I buried my face in my hands, through that muffled quiet, I heard a bird call from in the forest, a strange call, not like any bird song I knew, some strange European bird…"

As if on cue, a bob-white whistled from the dark treeline across the field behind the house. Paul, in the pale, blue-white light of the sodium-vapor lamp on the peak of the barn, saw the wetness well in Papa's eyes. Across the field, at Papa's house, the last light winked out.

Paul was awakened by voices arguing in the side yard. As he slipped on his jeans and sneakers, he recognized Papa's and Porter's voices, Porter's voice loud and slurred. Paul squeezed out the screen door onto the porch and saw Porter waving around an old carbine rifle as Papa tried to snatch for it.

"C'mon Ed, this thing's worth two hundred dollars," Porter said to Paul's father, "I'll let you have it for eighty."

"Give me that weapon, son," Papa hissed.

"Ed, you know that old Peterson down the road will give me a hundred for it in a heartbeat. I'm trying to give you a deal."

"I'm no collector, and neither is Peterson," Paul's father said evenly, "why don't you just give your daddy his gun back and go home and get some sleep. It looks like you had a pretty good time in town last night."

Paul's father grinned at Porter, like he was trying to be his chum, gave him a wink.

"The heck with you," Porter spat at Paul's father, "I'm getting me some money for this thing."

Paul had joined the men in the yard, and he could smell the whiskey on Porter's breath, and he could see his father's eyes narrow, the blood rise in his face.

"Porter, I'm going to ask you this just once. Take that rifle and get off my property."

"Ed, he don't mean anything by it," Papa pleaded, stepping between the two men.

"Leave now or I'll remove you myself."

"You ain't going to do squat. I'll leave when I'm good and ready."

Paul's father stepped around Papa, and Porter leveled the rifle at his hip.

Papa put himself between them again, his back to Porter.

"That weapon's loaded. I don't know if he knows it or not," Papa tersely whispered to Paul's father, "just go on in the house, and I'll take him home."

Paul's father stood silent for a moment, and then he backed up, reaching out with his hand, behind him, to feel for Paul.

"C'mon, Paul. Excitement's over."

"You'd better get. Ain't no one tells me what to do, mister," Porter slurred, waving the rifle, "you and that brat of yours. Maybe, Papa, you ought to just move over here. Live with somebody likes to listen to your old stories."

Papa kept himself between the rifle barrel and Paul and his father as they moved around the porch to the back steps. Porter stayed where he was, swaying slightly, but he kept the barrel trained on the three of them.

"Nobody tells me what to do," Porter repeated, his eyelids getting heavy, "especially not some old man or his goody friends."

Papa and Paul and his father stopped at the bottom of the steps, watching Porter's head begin to nod forward, the rifle sag from his grasp.

"Especially some old man who can't do nothing right," Porter mumbled.

Papa whirled toward Porter, his cane up in the air, like a sword.

"What did you say, boy?" Papa bellowed.

Porter, startled, swung the gun up, toward Paul and his father. In one instant, Papa, with an astonishing spryness, pivoted on his wooden foot and lunged through the air to shield them, and the rifle went off with a deafening crack. Papa fell hard at Paul's feet, and Porter dropped the gun and ran toward his house, stumbling across the field. Paul's mother rushed out of the back door and shrieked when she saw Papa lying in a crumpled heap at the foot of the stairs.

"Call an ambulance," Paul's father barked, and he knelt beside the old man, gently rolling him over to find the wound.

Paul, stunned, knelt also and cradled the old man's head. Paul gently brushed the dirt from Papa's forehead, and Papa, flinching from the boy's touch, opened his eyes.

"What happened," Papa asked, trying to raise himself on his elbow.

"Be still, Papa, we've got to find out where you've been hit," Paul's father said, frantically checking Papa's shirt for blood, "where does it hurt."

"The only place it hurts," Papa replied, "is my elbow where I fell on the concrete."

Papa sat up, slowly, and rubbed his arm.

"The Lord be praised," Paul's father said, "I think he missed you."

Papa felt up and down his chest, amazed, and struggled to get back up on his feet. Paul, as he pushed off the ground to stand also, caught a glint of metal out of the corner of his eye.

"Look," he said, as he picked it up from the ground in front of where Papa fell.

Paul held up a piece of lead, and he quickly dropped it because it burned his fingers. His father retrieved it and held it up in the sunlight. Papa slowly took it from Paul's father and turned it in his fingers. It was the rifle slug, flattened on one side as if it had hit something hard, like metal. As they looked closer, they could see, in the tiny scrapes on the side of the bullet that had flattened, traces of olive drab paint.

Melpomene's Garden

The horse's eye was wide with terror. Lauren knelt with one knee pressing the horse's heaving neck into the mud while the veterinarian, with her strong, sure fingers, probed along the horse's jaw up to its trachea.

"Hold her still," the vet admonished Lauren sternly, "you've got to keep her from hurting herself."

Lauren exerted more pressure on the horse's neck, until the frantic animal could no longer thrash. Lauren knew only the eyes of her grandfather's horses, all liquid brown and long-lashed as the animals nuzzled sugar from her flat palm. This eye, though brown, was ringed with panicked white, and Lauren was frightened. She turned her head and brushed sandy mud from the great muscle that swelled above the horse's foreleg. Lauren smoothed the short, silky coat so she would not have to see.

"That's right, calm her down," the vet said, quiet now, her voice soothing, "I think this old girl only had a scare."

Lauren looked up from the frightened beast, across a hundred yards of mud where other horses either struggled to extract themselves or lay motionless. In places, only legs and hooves protruded above the silt. Lauren realized that, only an hour before, this must have been a grassy meadow. Now it was an expanse of mud. A wide freshet, red, the color of clay, streamed down the middle, shallow enough to wade. Lauren looked behind her, at the school van, its doors flung open, ten feet from where the road disappeared beneath the shining silt. An hour before she had been on a field trip with her journalism class to observe the news teams covering the flood. Now they were all volunteers.

"This isn't the main deluge," Mr. Harris, her journalism teacher, shouted at his students, waving them to circle him, "This is just a horse pond that gave way on the side of that hill."

Lauren stayed with the frightened mare even though the vet had moved on to another animal. Lauren stroked the wide, muscular neck, and, under her touch, the horse calmed, the eye half-closed.

"Find out the topography," Mr. Harris yelled, gesticulating at the country-side, "interview any of these locals to get a description of the pond before it came down. Remember what the first news crew said about soil saturation this morning. This pond came down from the dam side being saturated with all the rain, not from the pressure of current. Find out how big the pond was. It must have been a pretty good size. See if you can find out in surface acres. Find out where the horse barn used to be. Estimate distances."

Lauren sat down hard in the mud when the chestnut mare suddenly struggled to her feet, and Lauren scrambled backward, expecting the horse to bolt. But the mare took a shaky step toward Lauren and nuzzled her long hair. When Lauren rose to join Mr. Harris, the mare nipped at her shoulder.

"See if you can find the owner of the horses," Mr. Harris continued, " Get a head count. See how many animals were killed, how many are going to have to be destroyed."

When two boys from her class ran past her and the mare, the horse nudged its long head under Lauren's arm until she held the mare across its withers. The mare kept its head bent to nuzzle at Lauren's other hand.

"If you aren't trying to get an interview, come with me in the van. We're going to drive back up the road to that store and phone in the story to the paper. We've scooped the big boys on this one. We got lucky."

Mr. Harris jogged across the mud toward the van, a broad smile across his face. Lauren was giving the horse a final stroke when a terrified whinny from across the field spooked the mare, and Lauren was jerked off the ground. Lauren fell at the mare's feet, and the horse shied away, its eye dilated with panic again. Mr. Harris was already starting the van motor. Lauren looked back across the mud to see the vet struggling with a huge black stallion, huge even buried to its flanks in the silt. Lauren struggled to her feet and raced to where the giant horse labored to free itself.

"Hold his head still," the vet commanded.

Lauren straddled the stallion's withers, her feet barely touching the ground even though the mud was to his shoulders. She leaned forward and took the massive neck in both arms, her face buried in his mane. The stallion thrashed and violently shook his head so that Lauren's face banged the bony point between his ears. Lauren felt her lip fatten, and her chin grew raw from the friction of his mane. Lauren hugged the great head as tightly as she could, pressing her cheek against one silken ear.

"Good," the vet panted as she tried to grasp his lower lip, "hold him tight."

The stallion continued to pitch his head from side to side, but Lauren held on like death. She could feel the supple spine and engorged muscles working between her thighs where she hugged him with her legs. She could feel each ragged whinny in the hollow of her chest, vibrate through the air in her own lungs. Lauren held him until he began to tire, and the vet, loosening Lauren's grip from around his neck, slid Lauren's hands down over the stallion's eyes. The huge horse quieted, and his long lashes tickled Lauren's cupped palms as he blinked. The vet skinned off her windbreaker and draped it over his forelock.

"This will make a better blinder."

The stallion relaxed in Lauren's grasp, and the huge head sank until his nostrils flared in the soft mud. Now it was Lauren who struggled to move the stallion. She cradled his head with both arms wrapped around his neck, her cheek resting on the windbreaker covering his eyes. Her back began to ache from leaning forward, holding the weight of the stallion's long head. She straddled him stiff-legged, and the back of her knees tightened and went numb. But the vet had rounded up a few men, and they began to dig out the animal with shovels, garden trowels, their bare hands, anything available. One man scraped back the silt with a board from the horse barn, and he was the first to unearth the stallion's left hock. When blood began to ooze up through the sotted soil, he discarded his board and dug with his hands too.

"Be careful," the vet warned Lauren, "when he starts feeling like he can get loose from the mud, he might start thrashing again."

But the stallion let his head remain limp in Lauren's aching arms. She cradled his throat in crook of her left arm, and, when that arm began to quiver with fatigue, she switched to her right arm. With her free hand, she stroked the huge beast, starting with his muddy nose, and then dropped her hand under his chin to smooth the loose skin there.

"Hey, doc," the man who discarded the board said, "come take a look at this."

The vet disappeared from Lauren's view, and, because of her struggle to hold the stallion, Lauren could not turn to see what the vet studied. There was a long silence. Then Lauren heard a wet slap across the stallion's flank, but the horse remained limp in her arms. Lauren didn't feel the stallion so much as flinch.

"Okay, go ahead and do it," the vet said after another silence.

Lauren felt the vet's hand on her shoulder.

"C'mon, honey. Lay him down."

Lauren suddenly realized what decision had been made, and she hugged the stallion with both arms, pressed her cheek into his long mane.

"C'mon, darlin', we can't help him any more."

Lauren hugged the huge head even tighter, felt one tear burn as it rolled down her cheek. A rough hand grabbed Lauren by the back of her belt and lifted her from the stallion. The horse's head dropped, muzzle-first into the soft mud, and Lauren saw the black barrel of a rifle swing up to the place where she had pressed her face against the stallion's silky ear. Lauren, struggling against the force that dragged her from the horse, cried out, and, at the sound of her voice, the black stallion, though blinded, raised its head from the silt and cocked its ears. Lauren spun to loose herself and sprawled flat in the slick silt. Before she could turn back to the stallion, a rifle crack split the air, the sharp concussion pressed her eardrums, the echo rang in her head. Lauren scrabbled to her feet, without looking back, and ran through the shallow freshet, across the mud and into the shade of the trees. She ran into the forest, stumbling and swatting branches as they clawed at her face, and, finally, collapsed at the edge of a small glen, because the running and the sobbing would not let her breathe.

When the jerking spasms of her sobbing subsided, and the canopied green of the glen sharpened out of blur when she blotted away her tears with her shirttail, Lauren became aware of a house at the other end of the clearing. Lauren hoped there was a telephone there, so she could call home, have her mother come to pick her up. There must be a road, Lauren reasoned, on the other side of the house, and she was relieved. She did not want to have to cross the washout again. Lauren picked herself up from the moss and moldy leaves and waded through the waist-high ferns to the door of the house, which was open.

"Hello," Lauren called into the house.

The house, Lauren noticed, was tidy and well-kept for a structure that seemed to have sprouted, like the ferns, from the mossy floor of the glen. Although Lauren stood before the front door, on a wide flagstone at the bottom of the small porch's two stone steps, she could see no path that led here. She turned in a circle and saw that even the ferns she had trampled to get here had sprung back, giving no indication of her passing. Lush vegetation grew right up to the house's foundation, and the house rose two stories up into the shady green of the trees' canopy. The house, Lauren guessed, was of Victorian design because the porch railings, the shutters, and the eaves, high in the green shadows, were webbed with fancy scrollwork.

"Hello, anybody home?" Lauren called again through the open door.

But still there was no response. Maybe, thought Lauren, whoever lived here had heard the commotion of the flood and had gone to help out. Lauren strained her ears to listen for any sound from the house, but her head still rang from the rifle's blast. Lauren climbed the steps and walked through the door, stopping just past the threshold. She was in a long hall that went to the back of the house. At the hall's other end, through the open rectangle of the back door, Lauren could see more abundant green, and flowers, a lavish confusion of color and shadow. To Lauren's right, a doorway led into a wall-papered room. Still straining to listen, Lauren ventured inside. Lauren immediately noticed the odd arrangement of the furniture: an overstuffed sofa and chairs, a coffee table with carved legs and marquetted top, an imposing armoire, all pushed to the center of the room and arranged there. The perimeter of the room was bare. No furniture was against the papered walls. Lauren, in her search for a telephone, circumnavigated the room at its outside edge, ending back at the doorway. Although she had seen no phone in her tour of the room, she had noticed, as she had circled and her eyes grew accustomed to the muted light from the draped window, that the flowered wallpaper was worn in a strange pattern. At shoulder height, all the way around the room, the paper was faded in a line a few inches high. Lauren turned to examine the wall beside the doorway, and she could see that the wallpaper, where there was no pattern, was beginning to show white. Where the line crossed over a printed flower, the design paled. Lauren stepped back into the hallway, and, although the hall was painted, she could detect the worn line where it had dulled the enamel's gloss.

"Do you have a telephone I could use?" Lauren called up the stairway.

The strange house was silent. Lauren continued down the hallway, to the next open door, on her left, beneath the carved staircase. In this room, the peculiar worn place was strikingly clear. The wallpaper was a floral design with chrysanthemum and peony blossoms raised in faux velvet on a ribbed satin field. Where the line circled the room at shoulder height, the nappy raised blooms had been worn as flat as the satin background, and as shiny. Again, no furniture encumbered the walls, and, in the center of the room, on carved marble pedestals, gathered the mute busts of men and women, mingling as at a disembodied dinner party. Lauren thought she recognized some of the statues. Was that Hamlet proffering Yorick's skull? Was the young girl who stared wistfully out of the half-draped window Anne Frank? Lauren walked into the frozen crowd and put her own face near the cold, marble ones. Each bust was dustless, immaculate. Each glowed with a filmy patina, as though polished by a person's palm.

From upstairs, Lauren heard a voice, a woman's voice, clear, coquettish, rhythmic, as if she were singing, or reciting. Lauren scampered back into the hallway, out from under the staircase, and craned her head up to glimpse a young woman descending the stairs. She wore a long gown, and, instead of holding the rail, she ran her fingers lightly across the wall, at shoulder height.

Lauren tried to speak, but she panicked, caught in this woman's house like a burglar. Lauren watched her dismount the staircase and run her hand along the wall until reached the open front door. The woman stopped and reached out for the opposite wall, placing her fingers on the worn spot, and then she turned and faced Lauren.

"I'm sorry," Lauren blurted, "I'm trying to find a telephone. I didn't know that anyone was home. The door was open..."

The young woman, her eyes closed, her pretty mouth downturned in an expression of exquisite sadness, made no response to Lauren's confession. Instead, she turned and entered the first room Lauren had explored. Lauren took a hesitant step down the hall, to follow her, when she heard the woman's voice, clear and melodious, resonate out into the hallway.

"The dying nightingale will cry tonight, its mournful song will echo through the glen. Then day will shaft its warmth down through the leaves, and silence her, her song lost like the night."

Lauren stepped into the doorway and watched the woman circle the room, her slender fingers gliding along the wall. Although the woman was silent now, the dying utterance of her words seemed to hover in the air, a sound like a wet fingertip circling the rim of a crystal goblet. The woman brushed past Lauren as she returned to trace her way down the hallway, and her long gown, as it billowed and slid past Lauren's fisted hands, was as soft as the stallion's ears. Lauren began to feel a deep pity well within her, as though the satiny touch of the gown had irritated a tender part of her soul, a part that yearned for things lost.

"From marble, I will fashion ornate vessels, to hold her vanished song, its liquid shape. And when the night returns, but she is gone, then I can drink from her exquisite sadness."

The alluring voice, with its crystal, lingering afternote, flowed out from the bust room, and Lauren moved toward it, with delicious slowness, down the hallway, as though she pressed through the delicate mass of a thousand hanging silken scarves.

"But can that quaff, so bittersweet, replace my nightingale, her quickened, feathered heart? No, no, this potion cannot sate my thirst. My vessel empties and my mouth is dry."

From the doorway, Lauren watched the young woman kneel in the center of the statues, her gown spread around her in soft heaps and folds. She caressed a sculpture which Lauren had not noticed before, a green marble carving of a stallion rearing, mane flying, hooves clawing.

"My child, is it the nightingale I miss? Is it her absence that has saddened me? Or is it me I suffer for, alone, bereft, and silent in the empty night?"

The woman turned her face to Lauren and opened her cataracted eyes. In a single, fluid motion, she rose through the mute assemblage, her arms outstretched, and cradled Lauren's face in her soft hands.

"The things we love and lose live on in us. Forget yourself, and you can give them life."

The woman took Lauren's hand and led her to the back door. There was no road, as Lauren had expected, but a riotous garden. The sun's rays slanted steeply through the green canopy as evening deepened, and Lauren descended the steps into the middle of the crimsons and mauves, the feathery golden petals of sunflowers and susans. Lauren looked back over her shoulder, but the doorway was empty. From somewhere in the house, Lauren could hear the melodious voice, its crystalline echo. Lauren moved through the nodding blossoms as though she were wading transparent, tingling water, the ghost of a deluge. She became aware of the rhythmic plod of her heart, and then sound resonated outside of her, faster, a distant gallop. The muffled beat of hooves on moss grew closer, filled up her chest. From the other side of a cloud of honeysuckle, a black stallion shouldered through the sweet-tongued blooms and snorted, his long-lashed eye half-closed and liquid brown. In the midst of the colorful rabble of flowers and the heady, perfumed air, he lowered his head to let Lauren stroke his porcelain horn.

The Killer Tattoo

Tim's heart beat hard in the back of his throat as he sat in the ratty barber's chair and watched the tattoo artist carefully adjust his gun. The dusty front window of the shop was illustrated with paintings of tattoos, garish dragons, lurid tigers gathered for a pounce, clumps of jabbering skulls, lewd naked angels, as were the walls inside, with pencil illustrations from floor to ceiling. The late afternoon sun slanted and projected the beasts from the window onto the brutes on the wall, and they writhed there, mingling together in a skin-crawling blur, oppressive layers of unspeakable creatures. Tim had come early on purpose. Everyone knew that this tiny storefront at the flea market on the edge of town was, as soon as the sun set, the haunt of bikers, ex-cons, a dangerous place even for dangerous men. But, even though Tim was alone with the scowling artist, the swirling, demonic menagerie on the walls seem to close in, and he felt the nauseating worm of claustrophobia turn in his gut.

"You know that this is going to last forever," the artist growled, and Tim clenched the tattered arms of the barber chair, unsure of whether the huge man meant the tattoo itself or the barbarous process of getting it.

"You're sure you know what you're doing, right" the artist said, glaring into Tim's pale face.

"Sure," Tim stammered, his mouth dry, his heartbeat ringing in his ears.

"Once I get started, there's no turning back."

"I'm sure I'm sure," Tim weakly chuckled, "go ahead."

"This mark will become part of you. You can hide it, but you can't hide how it will make you feel. You can't hide what it does to you."

Tim, as he looked into the tattoo artist's eyes, was speechless. A dark fire glowered in the bottomless irises beneath the giant's furrowed brow. The artist had the expression of a martyr or a passion-maddened saint. His gaze was both hypnotic and repulsive, as though he had gazed upon a beauty too terrible to experience.

"Give me your arm, then."

Tim leaned forward in the creaky chair, and the tattoo artist took Tim's thin bicep in his meaty hand. The artist's arms were tattooed solid from where the sleeve of his t-shirt ended down to his knuckles. The tattoos were snakes, coiling and wrapping around each other and his brawny arms, dozens of them. His arms were a slick mosaic of scales, and the back of each hand bore the spreading hood of a cobra. Tim was suddenly reviled by the sensation of being clutched by a grasping Medusa. The artist stepped on the footswitch, and the sputtering drone of the tattoo gun bored through the silence of the shop. Tim closed his eyes, unable to watch as the twitching needle approached his bare skin.

"Relax," the artist snarled, and he compressed the back of Tim's arm with one hand to tighten the skin on Tim's shoulder for the needle's penetration.

The whine of the electric gun slightly bogged as the needles entered Tim's flesh, and he had the sensation of being torn by a red-hot thorn. This had better be worth it, Tim thought, as he felt the artist firmly trace the outline of a heart circled by a scroll. This had better be worth all the times those boys that darken the door down at the pool hall taunted me and laughed and called after me as I walked past. Tim began to think of each chattering burn of the tattoo gun as a pain he would inflict on the pool hall crowd, Bo, Terry, Rod, and the rest of them. They all made noise about getting a tattoo, to show how tough they were, but none of them had ever so much as stepped foot in a tattoo parlor. Every second I endure puts me a second closer to showing them that I'm the real man, he thought. I'm the man with enough courage to come here alone and let them mark my flesh.

The tattoo artist deftly scribed the black lines beneath Tim's skin, working methodically, a hulking man who made his living driving fantasy and dream up under a person's flesh. Tim opened his eyes now and watched the artist toil at his shoulder. The whine of the gun, the thick scent of green soap, the light failing through the grotesque window all intoxicated Tim. With fascination he watched the illustrated madman labor over his skin. Tim saw him as a marvelous demonic accomplice in his plan for revenge on the pool hall boys.

"What name?" the artist grumbled.

"What?" Tim asked, startled from his vengeful reverie.

"Whose name do you want in the scroll?"

Tim's mind went blank. He had chosen this design because it had seemed simple. It seemed like a tattoo that could be done quickly. He hadn't thought of a name in it.

"Could you leave it blank?"

"Blank?" the artist barked, "a blank scroll means that the tattoo isn't finished. I always finish every tattoo I start."

"How about Emma?"

"Emma," the artist laughed, "who's that, your mother?"

Tim felt a hot flush rise up into his cheeks. Emma was his mother's name. The artist's laughter seemed to echo all the laughter that floated out of the pool hall, all the derision that followed his turned back as he ignored the bullies downtown.

"C'mon," the artist prodded, "what's your old lady's name?"

Tim didn't have an old lady. Tim had never had an old lady. Tim had never gone on a date because of his painful shyness.

"C'mon, chief, how many old ladies you got? Pick one of them."

"Angie," Tim blurted.

"That's more like it. How do you spell that? A–N–G–I–E?"

"That's right," Tim whispered, and even the act of someone asking him the spelling of Angie's name excited him. Angie was beautiful. Angie was perfect. Angie didn't even know Tim existed. She was a waitress at the poolhall by day and a dancer at the club outside of town at night. Once, she had come into the hardware store where Tim clerked and had asked for his assistance in picking out some bathroom fixtures, but Tim, imagining her in her bathroom, slowly disrobing for a long bath, had toppled the bathroom display, and his boss had sent him to the storeroom for a broom while another clerk helped her with her purchase. Now he only saw glimpses of her as he passed the pool hall, her high waist, her blonde hair, her long pretty legs that were accented by her short uniform. And most of the time, the pool hall boys blocked the doorway, hurling taunts and ridicule so that he didn't see her at all. His thoughts about Angie were like a smooth, thrilling stone he took out and caressed alone in his room at night when he could not sleep.

The tattoo artist slid his chair back and unclipped the tattoo gun from its long black cord. Tim looked down at his shoulder to see that the outline was finished, the heart welted around the black lines that formed it and Angie's name emblazoned on the scroll, one drop of blood welling from the bottom of the E. Suddenly, strangely, Tim felt her close by. He had the same sensation as the day she had entered the hardware store and had gracefully walked toward him, her beautiful legs scissoring, the shapely muscle of her calf plumping as she pivoted in her open-toed heels. The artist clipped on another machine and placed, on the table by the barber chair, two tiny thimbles of colored ink. He began with red.

Tim felt the needles differently now. Instead of a searing burn, the foolish result of some insane wish for torture, the needles cruelly stroked his thoughts of Angie, peeled back the dark skin of night and laid bare his dreams. As the artist colored the heart, the redness of the welted skin deepened to a brilliant blood red, and his thoughts of Angie deepened also. But the thoughts didn't seem to be fantasy as much as they seemed to be memory. As the heart darkened on Tim's shoulder, he became aware of details that had never existed in his fantasy: the taste of Angie's lips, the silkiness of the skin at the back of her knee, the way she smelled after a shower. When he thought of her now, it wasn't as a voyeur, some bashful kid who peeked in the pool hall at her from the sidewalk, but as a partner, a person familiar with her habits, her desires. Stranger still, he was overwhelmed with the feeling that she knew his habits, his desires. He saw himself as a different man, reflected in the mirror of her desire for him. Tim was oblivious to the crimson rake of needles under his flesh. A scene surfaced inside his closed eyes, a scene which he had never fantasized about, a scene of his wedding night with Angie. He saw the plush room, the heart-shaped bed, her long milky back as she turned from him and slipped out of her gown. Tim was no longer in the barber's chair but a motel room in Vegas. The luxurious events of that night welled up again, not fantasy but true memory, and Tim basked in each event, each pulse-quickening embrace. He relived the night from beginning to end.

"You're done, "the artist snapped, and he slapped a towel soaked with alcohol over the new tattoo.

The sting jerked Tim back into the present, the dingy, cluttered tattoo shop. Outside it was dark. Did I sleep through the end of that tattoo, Tim wondered. Tim handed three twenties to the artist.

"You'd better get out of here," the artist said gruffly, and the giant pierced Tim with a knowing glare, eyes that seemed to scour every corner of Tim's soul.

"What? Huh?"

"Your old lady is waiting out in the car, and, believe me, this is no place for a lady after dark."

Tim stumbled out the door and into the night. The moon was full, and, as Tim bent down to see who was sitting in the passenger seat of his car, he recognized the slender lines of the woman's neck, the profile illuminated by the moonlight. Tim slid into the driver's seat and slowly turned to stare at the woman who sat beside him.

"C'mon, honey," purred Angie, "let's go home and snuggle up."

As Tim drove Angie to work the next morning, he had trouble concentrating on the road. He was even too distracted to fully enjoy the way Angie sat next to him in the front seat, her hand resting on his thigh. When they had reached his house the night before, it wasn't the same house he had left, scared and desperate, on his way to the tattoo parlor. It was the same physically, his key still unlocked the front door, but, inside, his Spartan bachelor furnishings had been replaced with overstuffed sofas, lavender curtains. Doilies covered the coffee table and mantle. Delicate porcelain knickknacks crowded the top of a baby grand piano. When Tim nervously washed up for bed, nylons hung from the shower enclosure, and the bathroom smelled of perfume.

"There's a stop sign coming up," Angie shrilled, and Tim stomped on the brake.

"Uh, sorry," Tim stammered.

"What's wrong, baby? You're all tensed up."

"Nothing," said Tim, but, inside, he was afraid. He was on the threshold of a new world. So far, he admitted to himself, all of the changes have definitely been for the better. He tried to relax and smiled into Angie's concerned face. But he felt like a man recovering from amnesia. How would the pool hall boys treat him? They all had secret crushes on Angie, and now, he was her husband. Surely they would have to respect him for that.

Tim pulled down the alley behind the pool hall and parked by the back door.

"You don't have to walk me in, honey. I'm a big girl," Angie crooned, her lips teasing his earlobe.

"Oh, I just wanted to go inside and say hi to the boys."

Angie jerked back in the seat and eyes Tim suspiciously.

"What's going on in that head of yours today? You're acting like a different man."

"Oh, you know, change of pace..."

"Well, the bouncer doesn't come in until this afternoon, so watch out."

Tim got out of the car and held Angie's hand as she slid past the steering wheel and joined him. She took his offered elbow in both of her arms and leaned against him, her body soft and warm through the skimpy costume. Tim was glad for the support because his knees felt trembly. They walked down the back corridor, past the restrooms and, when they reached the dim, open pool room, they were greeted by a chorus of catcalls.

"Whoo, baby, lookin' good today," Bo hollered from the table by the front door.

"Great news," Terry shouted from the bar, "the owner said this place is going topless. Come over here and give us a preview."

Angie ignored them and slipped behind the bar and tied on her apron. Tim stood at the end of the bar, staring at his shoes, gripping the bar rail, his knuckles white.

"Shake a leg, Sweet Cheeks, we need another round up here at the table," Rod ordered, "and make last call for wimps."

Tim looked up at the table where Rod and Bo stood, and they were both smirking at him. Enraged, Tim stalked across the pool room. As he approached the pool hall boys, Bo swung up the butt end of his pool cue and prodded Tim in the sternum.

"Did we make the widdle man mad?" Bo whimpered.

"I've got something to show you cowards." Tim yanked up the sleeve of his dress shirt to reveal the tattoo. "What do you think of that?"

"I think," Terry said as he came up behind Tim and grabbed him by the upper arm, "that you got this out of a Cracker Jack box."

Terry rubbed his greasy thumb across the fresh tattoo and dropped Tim's arm when he saw a drop of blood well out of the heart and ooze down Tim's bicep.

"I think you got it in the wrong place," Bo said as he continued to tap the cue against Tim's chest, "I think it belongs on your butt with the words "Property of" tattooed above it."

The trio guffawed as Tim stood there, silent, his face white.

"I think I've never seen a worse case of jealousy in my life," Angie said as she swung in between Tim and the pool hall boys, nearly clocking B with a pitcher of beer," you're going to be late for work, honey. Wash up in back and then run on to work."

Tim hung his head and stared at his shoes again. He turned from the bullies and went to the restroom, disappointed that not everything had changed in this new world. As he wiped the soap from the tattoo, Angie breezed through the door and helped him.

"I don't know what got into you today. This happens every single time, but you've got to keep pushing it."

Tim hung his head at her exasperated tone.

"I don't know either. I thought maybe they'd respect me or something."

"Honey, those idiots out there don't respect anything except beer and Betsy Ross."

And, suddenly, Tim had an idea.

That night, after Tim dropped Angie off at the club, he drove out to the tattoo parlor again. As Tim pushed open the door, the tattoo artist looked up from the bench where he sorted needles with a magnifying glass and slowly shook his head from side to side.

"It usually takes a man a while to decide what he wants," the artist said. "I didn't think you'd be back so soon."

"I want the same thing I wanted last night, but I didn't get it."

"You got what you wanted," the artist growled, his eyes glowering, I always make sure that a customer is satisfied."

The huge man's beard twitched as he chuckled, and the sound reverberated around the cluttered room like thunder. Tim, suddenly, was afraid, unsure of his plan.

"Maybe I don't understand. Can you give me anything on these walls?"

"I can give you any *tattoo* you see on these walls. What you *get* is up to you."

Tim's eyes hungrily swept over the drawings. He wanted something that would make the pool hall boys respect him, something that even they would not mock.

"This one," Tim said, "I want this one."

Tim pointed to a bulldog's head. The dog wore a spiked collar, and underneath the image were the initials U.S.M.C.

"When did you serve?" the artist asked, "you seem kinda young."

"A couple of years ago," Tim lied, "right out of high school. I was in Iraq."

"A grunt, huh? Well so was I. "Nam, '66 to '70. Chopper gunner."

"I was infantry. We were the first unit in after the bombing stopped."

"So you saw combat? You know that dead taste you get in the back of your throat when all hell's breaking loose. You know how your head gets real clear when you can smell the enemy in the bushes, how you stick your buddy's dog tags in his mouth and move on."

"Yeah," Tim said, his voice close to quaking, "I know that."

"Or you will," the artist said under his breath as he clipped the outline machine to the electric cord, "you will."

As soon as the artist injected the first line under Tim's skin, Tim felt his mouth go dry, like sand. Tim closed his eyes and felt a burning wind blow particles into his face, stinging like needles. He choked on air thick with oil smoke. The drone of the tattoo gun became the chatter of distant small weapons fire. The shadows of bombers fled past the sand at his feet like a flock of monstrous birds. The pain where the artist toiled at his shoulder felt like a deep sunburn, and the sensation spread up the back of his neck, across his scalp under hos close-cropped hair. His groin throbbed from a thousand flea bites, and his thighs ached from running in loose sand. Tim was no longer in the tattered barber's chair, but the front of a jeep as it clawed along a desert road. Tim tried to open his eyes but was blinded by the noonday sun as it sat on his chest, sand blowing down his collar.

"You've got it," the tattoo artist whispered, and, again, he placed an alcohol-soaked towel over the fresh tattoo.

The chemical burn, invading the raw meat of his sore skin, was almost more than Tim could bear. Every nerve in his body was raw to the quick. Tim scrambled from the barber chair and sidled to the corner of the room, furtively glancing around the small room to make sure he and the artist were alone.

"Calm down, boy," the artist said as if he were soothing a skittish colt.

"How much..." Tim began, but the headlights of a car leaving the parking lot of the bar next door swept across the front window, like a spotlight, and Tim ducked behind the workbench, holding the back of his head with both hands.

"Sixty bucks. Now get the hell out of here before you hurt yourself."

Tim shoved the money at the tattoo artist and sprinted for the door. The raucous laughter of the tattoo artist followed him out into the parking lot as he fumbled to unlock his car door. When Tim left, his spinning back tires sprayed gravel against the dusty front window of the tattoo parlor.

Tim tried to calm down as he drove to the pool hall because he still felt very different; the panic that had welled up in him when the tattoo was finished had dulled into a rawness, his emotions on edge. Tim cautiously entered the pool hall and saw the pool hall boys at their regular table. Tim tensed as he walked past them.

"Well, if it isn't Sgt. York of the infantile platoon," Terry grunted.

"You mean Sgt. Dork, don't you?" replied Bo.

Tim reddened and felt his jaw cramp, like he was going to sob.

"Tim!"

Tim looked behind him to see old Mr. Loomis motioning him toward his table, the veterans' table, actually. Tim had never spoken to Mr. Loomis before. He was a WWII vet who had helped liberate the concentration camps. He never spoke about that experience though since he rarely spoke at all. Mr. Loomis usually nursed a single beer most evenings, but tonight Tim saw an empty glass before him in addition to the one he sipped from. Tim pointed at it as he sat down beside the old man.

"Dead soldier?" Tim asked with a grin until he saw the look of dismay flash across Mr. Loomis's face.

"That's an unfortunate expression, that is," Mr. Loomis whispered but then grinned himself, "never mind those punks. They don't know what it's like to serve."

Tim watched the trio and almost felt sorry for them when he thought about what Mr. Loomis had said. Tim, although this was his first ever conversation with Mr. Loomis, felt a strange camaraderie, a sense of brotherhood. The raw nerves that simmered in his gut eased a bit.

But just as Tim relaxed, Rod scraped a metal chair over to the table where the pair sat and slammed his mug down on the table.

"How is it that two men can be so different?" Rod mused as he looked at Mr. Loomis and then Tim. "How is it that one can be brave, respectable, a hero, and the other is just a weak, weak coward?"

Mr. Loomis looked at Tim to see his reaction, and there was none. Tim sat there and took the abuse like he always did. Rod let a stupid grin spread across his face and leaned back in his chair, tipping back on two legs. Mr. Loomis looked back at Rod and surreptitiously hooked the crook of his cane around the back leg of Rod's chair and yanked viciously. Rod flew backward and landed hard on the back of his head.

Bo and Terry walked over, but Rod had already scrambled to his feet, speechless in his fury.

"Show's over, boys," Mr. Loomis said under his breath, and the three bullies backed away.

Retreating, Rod said, "See what I mean. That old man has killer eyes. But Tim, he couldn't kill a fly."

And, as a single tear of rage formed at the corner of Tim's right eye, he had an idea. Tim brushed past the pool hall boys while glancing at his watch. It was 11:30. The tattoo parlor would still be open for a half hour.

"I've got a custom tattoo for you to do tonight," Tim blurted out as he entered the silent shop. The tattoo artist was reclining in the barber chair, ready to go home.

"Two tats in one day!" the hulk of a man jeered, "this had better be quick. I'm about to close."

"It won't take long," Tim replied, and then he took a deep breath.

"Well, what's this tattoo you want?"

Tim thought about his request. He almost said 'never mind.' But the memory of Rod's insult stiffened his resolve.

"I want a tear. A single tear beside my right eye."

The artist's expression went completely blank, and he let his huge hands fall into his lap. He looked down at the floor, and then he slowly, very slowly looked back up at Tim.

"You know what that means, right?"

"Yes, it means that I killed a man."

"You've never killed a man."

"You don't know that. What do I need, a court document saying I'm a murderer? Do I need my parole officer to write me a note?"

Tim's agitation annoyed the big man, so he raised his hand to silence Tim's harangue.

"If I do this tattoo, it will be last tattoo I ever put on you."

"Why? Am I not good enough for you to tattoo?"

Quietly, intently, the artist fixed his eyes on Tim's and repeated the exact phrase.

"If I do this tattoo, it will be the last tattoo I ever put on you."

"That's fine," Tim uttered with a wave of his hand.

So the tattoo artist inserted a liner needle into his gun and took a deep breath. Tim knew that a tattoo on his face would hurt and tensed, his hands white-knuckled on the arms of the barber chair. The tattoo artist stepped on the foot pedal and the drone of the tattoo gun filled the room. Tim flinched when the needle first penetrated the thin skin beside his eye.

"Sit still," commanded the huge inksmith.

Tim tried to relax, but, as soon as the outline was sketched out, he felt his chest constrict. Tim opened his eyes to see the artist change to the shader needle and then closed them again as the drone resumed. Tim could feel his chest constrict even tighter, and now he felt something compressing, restraining his wrists and elbows. As the tear was being shaded, the sensation tightened even more until Tim thought he could not stand it anymore.

Unclipping the tattoo machine from the wire, the artist said, "You're done."

Tim opened his eyes, but the hulking tattoo artist was not the person standing over him. He had been replaced by a doctor, and this doctor stood over Tim with a stethoscope and a syringe. Tim suddenly realized that the constrictions he felt were leather straps binding him to a gurney. His knees and ankles were strapped down as well. The strap across his forehead barely allowed him to see the large glass viewing window and the people gathered behind it, crowded together on folding chairs. Tim could see Angie on the front row, tears streaming down her face.

Suddenly a prison guard stepped up to stand beside the doctor and intoned, "For the murders of Bo Jones, Terry Held, and Rod Whitson, the state has sentenced you, Tim McGinn, to death by lethal injection. Do you have any final words you wish to speak to those gathered?"

Tim's throat was too dry to speak, but he croaked out a few sounds.

"What was that?" the guard said as he leaned closer.

"I didn't do it! There's been a mistake," Tim cried.

And then, from the corner of the room where the stainless steel cart held the needles and the vials of poison, a huge man with a demonic beard chuckled under his breath.

"That's what they all say," he said, "but that's a mighty fine tattoo."

Liar

Agrizzly drowsing in the spray of the trout-leap was Neddy Powerline, the migration's vibration crawling on the wind and under his skin. Jumpstarted by the Huge Twitdom, that dark era of American history where truth was daily mauled, the Great Migration drove hundreds of thousands of elderly hedonists rumbling northward each spring, encased in designer leather and straddling Harley tricycles like bobble-headed fetishing wannabees. They followed backroads through the great river valleys—the Mississippi and Arkansas—flooding north and westward toward the summer tent roosts that were cheaper than one bedroom flats on the beer-soaked outskirts of New Orleans and Memphis, the dreadfulness that became Shreveport. The Migrationers made do in flapping canvas, their bony asses luxuriously reclining on inch thick foam rubber mattresses unrolled on concrete slabs with a cooler full of lite beer icing in the 3 corner, the false bottoms loaded with cash. They nightly hooted along with classic rock and excited themselves with wild mockings of the truth, litanies of shit that never happened, tales too tall to walk through a door without bending over drastically and farting. And then these ancient bikers fled back south at the first hint of winter's tooth in their decrepit bones. So Neddy preyed on them. Neddy dozed in his hammock within earshot of the road as March thickened toward April.

Neddy thought of himself as a conservationist. He harbored black feelings against consumers glutting up the economy, and he found it his duty to thin the herd. He liked to use stealth and ten gauge wire cable. A mostly peaceful life in the far-out-of-town satisfied Neddy after the Huge Twitdom made suburbia a nightmare of property line disputes and discrimination lawsuits. Eventually no one could stomach the relentless carping and litigial expense over whose fence was on whose side of the line or whether brassieres blown into the side yard were on purpose or just accidentally hurtful. City-dwelling drove apartment owners to agoraphobic safe rooms for fear of squatters and their loud Puerto Rican attorneys, but they were still victims of the porch pirates and metalheads with earsplitting stereos. Once truth became subjective, all Neddy could do was abandon the peopled places to the biggest and best liars and carve out a homestead where neighbors gave him a wide berth because of rumors of missing meter readers or pollsters or hunters with a lousy sense of direction. Having a skull wash out of a stream at the edge of his property never hurt anyone. Most of the liars had just bought three-wheeled motorcycles and lemminged along.

Irony had lately consumed Neddy in a way that woke him at 3:14 in the morning when every empty room listened to the demented ticking of the grandfather clock. His workflow was a perfect circle. He waited for the second week of the migration, when the three-wheeled hordes 4 were a near-constant rumble on the horizon, and then, on a stretch of asphalt within walking distance of his house, he set up a cable between trees on opposite sides of the road—big trees, hundred-year-old oaks that had stood through ice-storms and tornadoes. This spot was at the end of a mile-long straightaway that suddenly swerved into several serpentine switchbacks. Neddy had perfected a triggered cam sprung with leaf springs and baling pulleys to instantly stretch a cable across the road at exactly four and a half feet off the roadway, the average height of the Adam's apple of both the rider and passenger on a Harley trike. Depending on the speed of the unlucky migrateurs, the trap would either clothesline them both off the back of the machine or loose their heads better than Robespierre had ever dreamed, their helmeted heads scooting and bouncing down the asphalt like leaky footballs. All Neddy had to do was collect their rides and their corpses before another wave of the elderly liars roared past. Then he would spray the gore off the motorcycle gear and stock it in the little shop he had set up at the other end of the straightaway. The sign out front of the log cabin saloon proclaimed "Last

Chance Supplies," and Neddy, with a punny relish, told all of the truthless coots that he recycled clothes and jewelry, parts, and engine liquids. All of these wrinkly truth-killers were both supply and demand.

World War I intrigued Neddy—particularly that brave son of Tennessee, Alvin York. Neddy had read that Sgt. York, as he waited in ambush for the German infantry to wind their way single-file to a good position, would pick off the last soldier in line, the way he had hunted turkeys back in the piney woods of home. The turkeys and the Mauser-toting soldiers wrapped in their winter coats, trench mud on their spiked helmets, never noticed their comrades fall behind them. Neddy would wait, hiding in the ditch-brush, until a great wave of bikers blew past, and then he would spring his wire on the last trike. Because the road immediately swung hard right, the last bike, now riderless, simply disappeared into an overgrown holler. In his first few 5 seasons, Neddy kept a secret hidey hole ready in case there returned a search party, but none ever had. He retrieved his winch and waited for dark.

Archeology was another of Neddy's wonderments. He would collect the belongings and memorabilia of his victims and note the quality of the goods, try to sleuth out their origins and worth. Turquoise was a tell-tale clue, filling whole display cases with rings and bracelets, bolos and belt buckles. These trinkets had come off snowbirds wintering in blustery tent cities on the crumbling concrete edges of Albuquerque and Tucumcari, whipped-up sand delicately coating the soft-serve above their cones. The leather was mute, all Chinese—produced, Neddy imagined, by short squinty cowboys who fed the cattle on formaldehyde and drywall—but t-shirts blabbed their hometowns. In the long off-seasons, Neddy alphabetized the shirts by the name of the motorcycle shop on the back logo. The names were mostly awful word plays like Horny Toad Harley, The Hog Farm, The Rowdy Beaver, and the artwork depicted lightning bolts and bosomy wenches having sex with skeletons. Neddy duly noted that his inventory of women's boots had more lefts than rights. This attention to detail one afternoon darkened Neddy's thoughts. He realized, as he examined an engraved pendant, that he had seen it before. Last year he had placed this same piece, a pitted sterling silver oval with a winged wheel embossed on it, on this same display tree. He flipped the pendant over and read the inscription, "Until the bitter end, be the last one in the wind." Biker doggerel. But Neddy chewed on the mathematical improbability. He harvested this necklace last year, sold it, and just harvested it again. For successive years, the last rider in a line had worn this piece of jewelry. Neddy's head was suddenly under a wave of paranoia, his ears and nostrils submerged in thick dread. Somehow this fact connected Neddy to these rolling 6 falsifiers. These fibbers on wheels shared an event, however insignificant, with him. He grabbed his Sharpie and marked the price on the tag up 200%.

***

And so the Migrations came and went. Neddy, like all competent traders, plied his skills as routine and weather allowed. He neither overspent himself in greed nor permitted want to pinch his lifestyle. His store stayed stocked with harvested parts. He invented Liar Day, a holiday to celebrate the end of the fall exodus and relieve the monotony between Labor Day and Halloween. But one day always dawned innocently and by evening washed him in serious distress—the day he reaped the pendant. For two decades now Neddy had yearly removed the pendant from a withered neck, or what was left of it, and restocked it in the back corner of his showroom, facing the wall in a spinning plexiglass display case. The damned thing was now priced at $500, but it sold immediately. Harpies obsessed with the flatness of the world pressed hundred dollar bills into his palm to have the pitted metal sway between their scrawny teats.

***

Neddy listened to the radio as he waited for a convoy of prevaricators to thunder past. The airwaves had also fallen victim to the death of truth. One of Neddy's choices was news shows trumpeting the virtues of the mouthbreathers in the government halls, passing raises for themselves while gutting rights for women. Every one of them raped a bit. The alternative was international pop with hideous synthesizers and Asian tongue yowling. On a clear day Neddy could twist in a pirate oldies station out of Brownsville, a megawatt station broadcasting ZZ Top 7 and Warren Zevon's grisly literate humor—can't you just imagine digging up the King, begging him to sing.

But a distant roar, just on the edge of Neddy's hearing, stopped him from fiddling with the transistor box. He quick-stepped, in a rehearsed and efficient parade-move, into his burrow in the ditch. He placed his right hand on the tape-wrapped handle of his liar de-rider. The grumble of motors slowly crescendoed until he could begin to hear individual bikes as they revved out of corners and burped and backfired into sharp turns. The awful Doppler of stereo speakers burbled Jagger complaining about not getting what he wanted. Then the first flash of chrome swung into view, and Neddy could feel the ground tremble with plentitude and bloody commerce. Neddy watched the horde glide toward him in its odd and stately fashion, practiced and precise as fezzy Shriners in a doomsday parade.

The lead trike rushed past, its backwash dangerously flattening Neddy's camouflage, and then another and another, the frenzied rip of rubber on asphalt mixing with the plexus-pounding of straight-piped V-twins. Neddy flinched as a gravel bounced off his goggles. He internalized the flow of the riders moving past in his diaphragm. He breathed their rhythm and let his lungs and the pistoned assault on his heart guide his trigger hand. If there were no apehangers, no Captain America sissy bar, he waited until his elbow's reflex smoothly loosed his mechanism; he watched, in the intimacy of the moment, the wire rise up from the roadbed; he followed the apex of the wire's whip gently deflect the tip of the windshield backward; he saw the cable flick down and catch between the rider's beard and collar; he saw the rider rise from his seat, arms spread Christ-wise, and he saw the rider strip the passenger off the back as they both vacated their sweaty ass-scented seats.

The trike, freed from its fact-raping endorsees, sped faithfully forward, riderless, until it disappeared in the Queen Anne's lace and low dogwood branches on the holler's edge. The couple lay motionless on the asphalt, somehow side-by-side and supine as if they were waiting poolside for some dapper Cancun waiter to bring them a margarita. Neddy lassoed the rider's ankles in a quick motion with his drag-strap, pulled him out of sight into the ditch. Neddy returned for the passenger, her right boot AWOL, and slid her behind him like a 55 gallon Glad bag full of styrofoam peanuts. She was a puff of nothing, completely hollowed out by disease or dessicated quietly by the wind, liar jerky. Neddy flapped open the body bag for the rider, rolled him in, and zippered the job done. Neddy knelt beside the passenger's body, unfurled another body bag in the pollen of the ditch bottom, and sneezed.

"Bless you."

Neddy found himself quickly on the edge of the ditch, a half-dollar-size pee-damp on the flap of his underpants. He looked down and saw the woman squinting at him through rheumy slits.

"What did you say?"

"Bless you, and thank you," she enunciated despite a bleeding and tipless tongue.

Neddy gritted his teeth and swallowed the impulse to bring his heel down between her eyes.

"You're the boatman."

"No."

"Yes. You're the one who takes us to heaven."

"Wrong."

Neddy stepped back into the ditch and listened intently. The rush in the pines' arms was a strong west wind.

"Sometimes we call you the Taker," she said. "We know you will take us quickly when we are ready to go."

"Shut up."

"The really old ones call you the Angel of Death. They say 'I Am hath sent me unto you.'"

Neddy palmed her skull and thumbed open her left eyelid.

"Look! I am completely pain-free. I am ready to move on to the pearly gates."

"Your neck is broken. You're not out of pain; you're paralyzed."

Neddy leaned down within whiffing distance of her rotting teeth and saw the pendant.

"Why are you wearing this?"

"That is the mystic neck piece, the sign that summons you, my ticket to the afterlife."

Neddy seized it, yanked it free, and shook it in the old woman's beatifically raised face.

"This is nothing. This is some Mexican junk you elderly dipshits spend your pensions on every year."

"It brought me to you. You've released me from the soul-searing pain I've vomited daily like a starving dog for seven years. You are a holy man."

"And you are a liar. You are confusing grace with homicide. You are like an old cat I once had. It wanted nothing to do with me until it got stinking, vile sores all over its belly, and then it wanted to jump up in my lap and ooze pus on my crotch as it died."

"Bless you that you've found me at last."

And Neddy thought about that. As in his sweaty dreams, individual faces rose up out of memory, seamed and toothless, the odor of Ben-Gay and Pearl Light stifling his nostrils. He 10 considered them pathetic felons, their ignorance condemning them to capital punishment. He inventoried the thousands of liars he had laid hands on like they were unwanted pets, their faces in his hands cold as kittens in a bucket of water. Sometimes the wind in their hair as they lay dead on the asphalt brought him tears. He remembered holding them, but they were the ones who would not let go. Suddenly Neddy loathed the human body's aggravating tenacity. This fortunate witch was the first one he had ever spoken to, and a sudden desire to interrogate her loomed in him along with a need to cover her face with a shop rag.

"How did you get this?"

"You gave it to me," she said.

"I did not. Tell me exactly how you got this."

"My sister bought it at your store. Last spring. She's got the cancer too."

Panic and rage quarreled in Neddy's gut. He was obviously part of a plot where he was more appreciated than implicated, and the notion sickened his large bowel.

"Two weeks ago my sister wore this pendant," the old woman continued, "but she made it all the way to Spokane. She mailed it to me last week. I was hoping to have better luck."

"Luck," Neddy chortled, "you are a victim. You don't know how this whole monkery works."

The old woman welled up, her eyes shining with betrayal. "Yes, I do. The poem tells it. You know the poem tells it. If you want to end it all, then be the last bike in the line. You'll be taken somewhere in this ten mile stretch of road if your dream comes true."

"Dream? That's some sick liar joke."

"You have taken away my pain. For that, I love you Neddy."

Neddy's rectum puckered as he remembered the long arm of the law, the sheriff's big dumb moon face at his front door, so he reared back and slung the pendant as hard as he could across the road.

"No," the old woman screeched, "no, no, no! You have to put that back in the store! You have to. You have to! There are others depending on you."

Neddy studied how she sobbed and wailed in the ditch-bottom, motionless save her ratcheting jaw and rolling eyeballs.

"Please put it back," she pleaded, blood dribbling her chin, "please. Please."

"It's gone."

The elderly suicide queen burst forth with a new volley of shrieks. She keened like a virgin in labor. She made the dead-center of Neddy's brain hurt, and he thrashed about on the roadside.

"Shut up!"

"Please find it and put it back. Please!"

"It's nothing."

She said, "It's all we've got."

And, those words spoken, she quieted. She looked like a plastic baby Jesus kidnapped from a crèche then abandoned by stray dogs. So Neddy knelt beside her and slid her onto his lap. Far away he heard the next wave of bikers swarming. He cradled her head against his chest. He listened to her breathing steady toward sleep as he held her, and then, as she started to gently snore, he hugged her hard into his chest until his arms trembled and she was completely silent in his embrace.

***

Neddy burned down his store on Liar Day. He watched the flames frolic and lick, and the smoke billowed so thick and black that the yokels from the volunteer fire department eventually showed up in their pickup with the half empty water tank sloshing in the back. Neddy watched from the woods as they surveyed the job then shrugged their shoulders and went back to the station to kill caged possums with a nail gun.

The brush hogs might have flung it anywhere; a raccoon could be miles away washing it at the mouth of some cave-stream; a local nerd with a metal detector may have given it to his one-armed sister. It could have washed out to sea. Neddy was through with harvesting. The next time a growling knot of hoary motorbikers passed, they saw Neddy walking the road edge, his head down and studious as Walt Whitman hunting aluminum cans.

The Plays

THE CORNER OF VICTORY AND VAN NUYS

A play in one act

CHARACTERS

RALPH: Biker tattoo artist, early 30's, artist and cynic.

CHARLIE: Vagabond in his late 60's who is working his way south as the winter comes on.

DANNI: Under aged runaway, a worldly 15-year-old.

POLICEMAN: Twenty-something beat cop.

SETTING

A run-down row of storefronts in the San Fernando Valley (Los Angeles) suburb of Van Nuys.

TIME

Early evening. The week before Christmas. The eve of a freak cold front.

<u>SCENE</u>

Two storefronts with a wide but dead-end alley between them. The store front at stage right is a tattoo parlor with a door and a large front window. The storefront at stage left is boarded up. The alley is empty except for a makeshift bench of crates and cardboard against the side of the boarded-up store.

(CHARLIE slowly enters from stage left, investigates the alley, and sits on the crates. He slips off a rucksack and lays a pile of newspapers that he has been carrying under his arm onto the bench beside him. RALPH, who has been standing in the large front window of the tattoo parlor, notices CHARLIE and steps out the door onto the sidewalk.)

RALPH

Whoa, Buddy! This ain't no bus stop.

CHARLIE

Don't worry, friend. I'm not movin' in.

RALPH (annoyed)

This is my *business, friend.* People start getting off work right now, and I don't need 'em to see no bum convention outside my front door.

CHARLIE

I promise I won't pester any of your patrons.

RALPH

Just *looking* at you will run 'em off. I'm serious; you need to beat it.

CHARLIE

A little pity, friend? I've been walking all day and need to take a load off. Maybe I'm the angel come to give you a lottery ticket.

RALPH

I ain't your friend, you ain't no angel, and if you don't beat it I'm calling a cop.

CHARLIE

Go ahead! I don't see any "No Loitering" signs.

RALPH

(reaches inside the door for a baseball bat)
I don't see any "No Battering" signs either.

CHARLIE (tiredly)

C'mon, then. I'm a little worn out, but I've got enough strength left to kill a man who's messing with me.

RALPH (suspiciously)

What?

CHARLIE (angrily, posturing for a fight)

C'mon! What are you waiting for? An invitation? I just gave you one. It's been a while since I've felt a jaw crack under my knuckles.

RALPH

Huh?
(RALPH is hesitant to move toward CHARLIE, and then a tone signaling an update from an app sounds from his back pocket. RALPH tucks the bat under his arm and pulls out his phone)
Hold on. I got a weather update.

(pause while the app loads up. RALPH is intent on the results as CHARLIE looks around the alley.)

Hoo, Buddy! It says that we're supposed to get a freeze tonight! We got the little warning exclamation point and everything! What's up with that!?

CHARLIE

Global warming, I guess.

RALPH

Global warming? That sounds more like global cooling. I don't ever remember a freeze this time of year in L.A.

CHARLIE

So it's usually a lot warmer then?

RALPH

Oh yeah! Most Christmases I sit out back and barbecue in my shirt sleeves, pick a few oranges, work on my tan. (Pause) Where you from, man?

CHARLIE

Up north. I've been travelling for a while.

RALPH

Where up north? Frisco?

CHARLIE

Not California.

RALPH

Back east? Chi-town? The Great-freakin' Lakes? Hey are you from *New York City*? (pronounces it with a Texan drawl like the Pace salsa commercial)

CHARLIE

No, just somewhere else.

RALPH

Well, Mr. Mystery, if you won't tell me where you're from, then where're you going?

CHARLIE

I'll know when I get there.

RALPH

You'll know when you get there. Hmm. I call BS.

CHARLIE

I'm close. I think. See, I don't need a gadget to tell me about the weather. I have my knees and elbows that go stiff when the birds go south. I have my spine that feels the ground get hard.

RALPH

Yeah, life's rough, dude. Why don't you get a job?

CHARLIE

There's things more important than jobs.

RALPH

Yeah? Like what?

CHARLIE

Knowing things.

RALPH

Knowing things? What the hell do you know?

CHARLIE

Insulation.

RALPH

What?

CHARLIE

How to keep warm. Think about it. The temperature in the universe goes from near absolute zero in deep space to trillions of degrees at the heart of the sun. But we naked apes only survive in a range of less than a hundred. Even your dog can shiver through a night in the twenties. If that were you, you'd be dead.

RALPH

So now you're going to give me the bum tip of the day?

CHARLIE

Newspaper. In layers.
(He rummages through the pile of newspapers)

CHARLIE (continued)

Particularly the Sunday edition—the book review.
(He begins stuffing newspaper up each pant leg)
And the best pages are the poems. Look, I've got Miller Williams and Mark Doty up this leg and Emily Dickinson and Billy Collins up this one. Poems keep a person a lot warmer than the news.

RALPH

Who the hell are they? Famous?

CHARLIE

Yes! Wonderful poets. People you should know.

RALPH

Hey, I know famous people, man. Did you know that I'm friends on Facebook with both Dave Navarro and Jesse James?

CHARLIE (Shocked)

Jesse James?!? That can't be!

RALPH

Whattaya mean?

CHARLIE

He's dead!

RALPH (truly concerned)

You're kidding me, man. How?

CHARLIE

Robert Ford shot him in the back of the head!

RALPH

Who? When did this happen?

CHARLIE

1882!

RALPH (relieved and disgusted)

Geez, you're out of it, dude. I'm talking about the bike builder; you know, the guy that was married to Sandra Bullock.

CHARLIE (dumbfounded)

Bike builder? Jesse James was an outlaw.

RALPH

Whatever.

Deep space, newspapers... I think you're confused, old man.

CHARLIE

Me confused? You're the person doodling on people's hides. Giving each one a permanent fad.

RALPH

It's called skin art.

CHARLIE

Art? What artist ever chose a rotting canvas? What sculptor worked on a crumbling stone?

RALPH

You don't get it, man. Tats are forever.

CHARLIE

Forever? All of your art will one day be put in a box and buried in the cold, cold ground. Or it'll wind up in a furnace; your masterpiece will be smoke that coils out an industrial chimney.

RALPH

Excuse me, Mr. Critic. Enlighten me as to the nature of true art.

CHARLIE

Aristotle said, "The aim of art is to represent not the outward appearance of things, but their inward significance." That could be words. (pause) Images in stone. Deeds, perhaps.

RALPH

But not ink, I take it.

CHARLIE

Not like poetry. What, for instance, does that star on your forearm mean?

RALPH

That's my beacon of hope. I got that when my mom beat cancer for the first time. She got a double mastectomy, and she got stars tattooed where her nipples used to be. This star is just like those.

CHARLIE (in a conceding tone)

So that may be art after all. Not because of the design—I thought you may have been a sailor—but the deed. Art communicates. Art is shared.

RALPH

So is ink art or not?

CHARLIE

Who knows? Perhaps it is. Maybe it's all in the appreciation.

RALPH

Make up your mind.

CHARLIE

It's not called "making up your mind." It's called "learning."

RALPH

It's getting cold out here. Later.

(RALPH goes back in the store and kicks back in the barber chair in the front window. CHARLIE finishes stuffing his clothes with newspaper and then fastidiously arranges the newspapers in layers on the crates, as if he were making a bed. He gathers all of the collapsed cardboard boxes from the back of the alley and then sits on the crates and fishes a locket on a chain from beneath his shirt. He opens it and gazes at a picture within. He kisses it, closes it, and replaces it beneath his shirt. He then arranges the boxes over him expertly, almost disappearing on the crates. DANNI enters stage right, hesitantly walks past the tattoo parlor and stops at the mouth of the alley. She's wearing jeans and a hoodie, carrying an oversized bag. She seems tired and moves toward the crates where CHARLIE is lying down, and she unknowingly sits on his legs.)

CHARLIE

Hey!

DANNI

(bouncing right back up onto her feet and running a few steps away)

What're you doing, scaring people like that?!

CHARLIE

Didn't expect the furniture to talk back, huh? I'm sorry, no social butterfly, me. I'm more of a social chameleon. I have a way of blending in with my surroundings.

RALPH

(enters out of the tattoo parlor and stands close to DANNI)

Hello, little lady! Step into my parlor...

CHARLIE

...said the spider to the fly.

DANNI

(to RALPH)

Cool it, Romeo. I'm not looking to be the next Kat Von D.

RALPH

But you got it going on with the Gap and the Gucci, baby. You aren't a model, are you? Didn't I see you in a Sears ad in the Beverly Hills paper?

DANNI

Try Armani and Ellis. I'm not interested in your zip code.

CHARLIE

Wonderful brands all. I prefer Goodwill and Salvation Army, though, for that lived-in look.

RALPH

So, you want to come in and warm up? Sit in a comfy chair and listen to some tunes?

DANNI (suspiciously)

What do you want?

RALPH

Calm down, little darlin.' Why are you making me work so hard to be the nice guy? I could leave you out here with the walking dead.

CHARLIE

Interesting choice he gives you—walkers or stalkers.

DANNI

Is there someplace inside where I could charge my phone? My battery is completely dead.

RALPH

Of course there is. Just come on in and get comfortable.

CHARLIE

Yeah, but is there going to be a charge for the charge?

RALPH

Butt out, old man.

DANNI

I'm supposed to meet a friend near here, but my phone died, so I can't use my map app.

RALPH

Not your boyfriend is it?

DANNI

Somebody I met online. He's a junior at Van Nuys High. We met in a chat room right after Halloween.

CHARLIE

You ever seen him in person?

RALPH

Hey, you better watch out! I bet he's some middle-aged pervert with a basement full of chains and a camcorder.

DANNI

Would you two mind your business? Don't you think I can take care of myself?

CHARLIE

What are you running away from?

DANNI

Who says I'm running away?

RALPH

Your lame story, for one thing. These streets will swallow you whole, sister. All the cops will find of you one smoky Saturday night will be that Gucci bag hanging out of a dumpster.

CHARLIE

Can't you go back home?

DANNI

Would you two get off my case? What makes you think I have anything I want to go back to?

CHARLIE

I bet you've got family that's worried about you.

DANNI

Yeah, right about now the nurse is changing Mom's diaper and getting the IV ready, and dear old stepdad Fred is wandering the upstairs hall to see if he can catch an eyeful of me changing out of my school clothes.

RALPH

What's wrong with your mom?

DANNI

What's it to you? Are you going to let me charge my phone or not?

RALPH (insistent)

What's wrong with your mom?

DANNI

Forget you. It's none of your business.

RALPH (more insistent)

What's wrong with your mom?

DANNI

Brain cancer, okay?! Happy now!? Got your nosy fix!?

CHARLIE

They've probably got cops looking for you.

RALPH

So you're turning your back on your mom because she's got cancer?

DANNI

My mom wouldn't know my back from my front.

This past Easter we found her sitting in her Sunday dress on the double yellow line on Sepulveda Avenue. Two lanes in both directions were honking like crazy, but she was looking at something way past anything we could see. She'd been losing weight for months, and that morning cancer came and gave her the gifts of the long stare and a pink ribbon.

RALPH

You owe her. You need to go back and help her.

CHARLIE

If you really want to leave, I mean really run away for good, we need to make sure that the cops don't find you.

RALPH

Leave? She needs to go back home and do everything she can to make sure that her mom knows that she loves her. She needs to be changing those diapers and holding her hand in the bathtub. She needs to be listening to her breathe at night. She needs to hold her when her breathing gets hard.

DANNI

She *was* home, and now she's gone. She's a husk rattling in a bony basket. Home is a bunch of empty rooms with loud clocks on the walls.

CHARLIE

Leaving is hard, too. If you decide to run away, you have to get your mind around the idea that you'll never go home again.

DANNI

Never?

RALPH

You talked about deeds, old man. Isn't honoring your mother a deed?

CHARLIE

Never.

RALPH

Here, use my phone. Call home. Let 'em now where you are.

CHARLIE

If you leave, you'll be sitting on a park bench somewhere, hoping it won't rain, watching seagulls scuffle over a Big Mac wrapper when they put her in the ground.

RALPH

You're not going to walk away from her when she needs you. She's not in the ground yet.

CHARLIE

If you leave, all your kin will remember you as an empty folding chair by an open grave.

RALPH

Yeah! You gotta have other family! Aunts, uncles, grandparents! Get hold of them.

CHARLIE

If you leave, there will be two beds in your house that won't have anyone in them anymore.

RALPH

I've got my bike out back. I'll get it and take you home. We'll ride back home together. We'll take care of things.

CHARLIE

You'll work at not missing her. You'll go to the beach for the warm wind, and you'll hear the sea's voice. And that voice will fill you up, just like her voice used to.

RALPH

Shut up, old man! Just shut up!

DANNI

She can't call my name. She doesn't know my face anymore.

RALPH

Yes! She can! All you need is to give her another chance!

CHARLIE

No, child. She is becoming the sea. She is beyond knowing you. She is a force that carries on beyond your caring. You can sit at her shore, but she ebbs and flows with the moon.

RALPH

Stop listening to this nonsense. Your mom will always know you. You need to be holding her bony ass in your lap, stroking the bandanna covering her bald head, promising her one more Christmas.

CHARLIE

You think that if you leave you will be rid of all that, but it will follow you like a stray dog; it'll lean up against you to get warm when you sleep at night.

DANNI

It just has to stop.

RALPH

Any life is better than no life. Don't you get it? You've only got so much left.

DANNI

It just has to stop.

CHARLIE

She'll move into your dreams.

DANNI

Don't *you* get it? *She* has already left *me*.

RALPH

She didn't leave you! She's being taken!

CHARLIE

She's not choosing tonight. *You* are.

DANNI(to RALPH) (desperately)

Can I charge my phone? Stay a while?

RALPH

You go home. Tell me where you live, and I'll make sure you get there.

DANNI

C'mon, man, be cool. I'll keep you company.

RALPH

What do you mean, keep me company?

DANNI (in a sexy voice)

I'll be your girlfriend tonight. We can stay warm together.

RALPH

You don't even know how stupid that sounds. You're on your own, kid.
(RALPH exits into the tattoo parlor, locks the door behind him, and shuts

off the interior light.)

CHARLIE

There is going to be a killing frost tonight. The mercury is dropping in the mouth of a dying day.

DANNI

Everything will be alright. I've been on my own before.

CHARLIE

What, a slumber party? Camping in the backyard? (pause; he soothes his tone)

Is your Christmas tree up already?

DANNI

Since Black Friday.

CHARLIE

What's under the tree? What'd you give her?

(DANNI turns away and sits on the steps of the tattoo parlor.)

I knew this man once. He had a daughter a little older than you, and he gave her everything she wanted. Her mother left him before the girl could remember, and the man bought her stuff, clothes, puppies, a guitar, a horse. But the girl was wild, like her mother, and one day she came home and asked the man for something he wouldn't give her, an abortion. The girl had a boyfriend who'd quit school and worked at the steel mill, and the two of them wanted to ride his Harley out to Denver, hang out in Rocky Mountain Time, build a cabin. But the man said no, and he locked her in her room, forced her to have the baby. He found the boyfriend in an alley one night and beat him so bad he never came back. Six months after the baby was born, the daughter came down to the kitchen table one night where the man was drinking whiskey, too much whiskey then, and she said that if he loved her he would give her one thing, this one last thing, and she would never ask again. All she wanted for him to give her was some space, some time, that she'd be back for the baby when she could. And he passed out, and she was gone, and he missed her for a long time, years, more Christmases than he could count on both hands, but she came back one day. She showed up on the porch one May morning as a soft rain began to fall, and she asked for her daughter, but the man had given her away. That was the last time he ever saw her. (pause)

CHARLIE (continued)

Do you have something from your mother under the tree?

DANNI

I don't deserve a gift. (pause)

That man was you , wasn't it?

CHARLIE

You don't get to choose what you deserve.

(DANNI exits stage right. The lights dim, and CHARLIE watches her go then arranges the cardboard carefully over himself. He settles in, and the lights almost completely fade. Several long beats after CHARLIE has lain still, DANNI enters stage right and slowly moves to the door of the tattoo parlor. She looks around and then quietly raps on the front door. She waits. She raps again, but there is no answer. DANNI sits down on the steps of the tattoo parlor and pulls her hoodie around her. She puts her bag on the threshold of the doorway and lays her head on it. FADE TO BLACK.)

(After a significant pause, the lights slowly come back up. It is the next morning. CHARLIE is lying uncovered on the crates, rigid and still. Enter POLICEMAN from stage right. He walks slowly, examining what appears to be a pile of cardboard in front of the tattoo parlor, but then he moves past to CHARLIE. He examines him carefully, trying to rouse him by shaking his shoulder.)

POLICEMAN (into a walkie-talkie)
  EMT one- niner, do you copy?
  (staticky and inaudible reply over the radio)

POLICEMAN
  I've got a deceased elderly male that needs to be taken to the morgue.
  (staticky and inaudible reply over the radio)

POLICEMAN (continued)
  Copy that. I'll meet you at the corner of Victory and Van Nuys with directions to his location. I'd stay with the body, but I've got a runaway I'm looking for and more homeless to check on.

(POLICEMAN exits stage left.)

The pile of cardboard in front of the tattoo parlor shifts and moves. DANNI appears from beneath. She looks around the stage in a bewildered manner, pushing away the cardboard and newspapers that have covered her away. She looks over to CHARLIE and gazes at him for a long while. Then she notices a locket on a chain around her neck and lifts it up, opening the locket. She looks at the pictures inside. The static of a police radio sounds offstage stage left, and DANNI quickly rises and exits stage right.)

DUKE SIMS AND THE DUCHESS OF RUSSIA

A play in 1 act
<u>CHARACTERS</u>

MRS. NOVAK: Agoraphobic immigrant widow in her 60's.

VINCENT: Paper boy who is 12 years old whose parents are divorcing.

SYLVIA: VINCENT'S little sister.

TYLER BROTHERS: Two neighborhood boys who torment VINCENT, aged 11 and 14.

RADIO ANNOUNCER

<u>SETTING</u>

An apartment building interior in Cleveland Heights, Ohio.

<u>TIME</u>

The summer of 1969.

<u>SCENE</u>

The doorway of MRS. NOVAK's apartment. The doorway is in the middle of the stage facing perpendicularly to the audience. Stage left is the hallway with a doorway to the service stairs in the rear and a window to extreme stage left. Stage right is the interior of MRS. NOVAK's sparsely decorated and simple apartment with a bed far stage right, and a table and chair. All of VINCENT's and MRS. NOVAK's conversations take place through the closed door. The first transitions should have a rhythm indicating the routine of the interaction and the passage of months.

(Lights up. VINCENT enters breathlessly from the service stairs door and walks to the doorway. He is dressed in a jacket and cap, and he carries a canvas newspaper bag over his shoulder. He has a coin changer on his belt. He knocks at the door.)

VINCENT

Newspaper collection!
  (MRS. NOVAK is sitting on the edge of her bed wearing a black mourning dress and a black hat with a veil. A radio plays in the background broadcasting the seventh game of the 1968 World Series game. The announcer describes Jim Northrup hitting a triple against Bob Gibson.)

RADIO ANNOUNCER
  Tony, it's hard to believe that it's already the seventh game of the 1968 World Series, two out, top of the seventh. Norm Cash limbers up and digs in against Bob Gibson. Cash has a jawful of Juicy Fruit and is working it hard in the batter box. He reaches for a an outside ball-strike one. (Pause) Gibson winds up and follows through—ball one—also outside and low. The sun is shining, and the temp is in the mid-sixties here at Busch Stadium in St. Louis, a beautiful afternoon for a baseball game. Gibson shakes off a sign, then another. He throws and misses the zone just high and outside for ball two. Gibson winds up and snaps a dandy of a curve ball into the top of the strike zone for strike two. Two balls and two strikes. (Pause) Gibson takes the first sign and throws another curve ball but low. Bob Gibson hasn't walked anybody today. He's struck out seven and allowed an infield hit to Mickey Stanley in the top of the fourth. Full count, two out. (Pause) Cash zeroes in on a fast ball, and it's a line drive to right field, base hit. (Pause) Up next is Willie

Horton. Horton is a dangerous hitter and strong enough to hit anything out of the ball park. Gibson pitches from the stretch and throws a curve ball low and outside, base hit! The Tigers are threatening now with two outs, base hits by Cash and Horton. Up next is the grand slam kid, Jim Northrup. He clobbered the Cardinals in the last game in the top of the third against Washburn. He's had two homers and six RBI's in this series. He's one out of nine against Gibson, and that was a homer. That's the only run that Gibson's permitted in this series. McCarver runs out to the mound and makes a quick exchange with Gibson. Gibson whips one in from the stretch, and Northrup slams a high fly ball! Center fielder Flood almost fell–he came in and then had to reverse direction, misjudged it over his head! Two runs are going to score! Flood grabs the ball on the warning track and throws it to the cutoff man in shallow center. Jim Northrup almost misjudged one like this earlier in the game, and now it's happened to Curt Flood, a Golden Glove center fielder! As he started for the ball, something caught his spikes, and he nearly went down! He had to settle for watching the ball sail over his head to the warning track, something that rarely happens to a centerfielder of his caliber! The Tigers now have two runs in the seventh. This all came after two out, a full count, and nobody on. So Detroit leads, two to nothing. They're nine outs from winning the World Series!

(She doesn't respond to VINCENT's knock.)

VINCENT waits, intent on the radio broadcast, then leaves a newspaper on her threshold and walks to the window where he peers intently outside, looking for people below, still listening to the broadcast. FADE.)

(Lights up. VINCENT enters breathlessly from the service stairs door and walks to the doorway. He is dressed in a heavy winter coat, and he carries a canvas newspaper bag over his shoulder. He knocks at the door.)

VINCENT

Newspaper collection!
(MRS. NOVAK is lying in bed. A radio plays the news in the background.

She doesn't respond to VINCENT's knock. VINCENT waits for a few seconds, leaves a newspaper on her threshold, and walks to the window where he peers intently outside, looking for people below. FADE.)

(Lights up. VINCENT enters breathlessly from the service stairs door and walks to the doorway. He is dressed in a spring jacket, and he carries a canvas newspaper bag over his shoulder. He has a coin changer on his belt. He knocks at the door.)

VINCENT

Newspaper collection!
   (MRS. NOVAK is sitting at the table. There is no radio playing. She rises and takes an envelope from the table and slips it under the door. VINCENT takes the envelope.)

VINCENT (continued)
   Thanks!
   (VINCENT leaves a newspaper on her threshold, walks to the window where he peers intently outside, looking for people below. FADE.)

(Lights up. VINCENT enters breathlessly from the service stairs door and walks to the doorway. He is dressed in shorts and a tee shirt and a ball cap, and he carries a canvas newspaper bag over his shoulder. He has a coin changer on his belt. He knocks at the door.)

VINCENT

Newspaper collection!
   (MRS. NOVAK is standing by the inside of the door. She holds an envelope in her hand, but, when she bends down to slip it under the door, she begins to cough violently.)

VINCENT (continued)
Are you okay in there?
(MRS. NOVAK slips the envelope under the door.)

VINCENT (continued)
Thanks!
MRS. NOVAK (through the door)
Wait! Who won the ballgame yesterday?

VINCENT
The Indians. Sam McDowell threw a three-hitter against the Yankees. Duke Sims got a double. It's all in the sports section.

MRS. NOVAK
And today? Is there a game today?

VINCENT
Yeah, we're still in New York. It's listed on the front page of sports.

MRS. NOVAK
When are we back home?

VINCENT
Tuesday. We've got a home stand against the Twins. Don't you listen to the radio?

MRS. NOVAK
It has broken.

VINCENT
Then read the schedule in the paper. Here it is. Open the door.

MRS. NOVAK

No! Just leave it on the step.

VINCENT

You know how to read the schedules, right?

MRS. NOVAK

I read the mother tongue. I never learned to read the English very good.

VINCENT

Then why do you get the paper?

MRS. NOVAK

For the pictures! Lining the canary's cage! Why so many questions? You the secret police? (Pause) And what about you? Why are you always out of breath when you come here? Are those stairs too much for you?

VINCENT

The stairs are okay. It's getting to them that winds me.

MRS. NOVAK

What are you talking about?

VINCENT

The Tylers.

MRS. NOVAK

Who are they?

VINCENT

Two brothers. A couple of goons who can't pass sixth grade. They live over on Pennfield, and they listen for me to put their paper inside the storm door, and then they chase me here.

MRS. NOVAK

Goons? What are those?

VINCENT

Knuckledraggers. Bullies.

MRS. NOVAK

Oh, Bolsheviks, you mean. You run that whole long block with all your papers?

VINCENT

I have a key to the back service stairs of the building. I can beat them here and get in the door before they get me. I can lock them out.

MRS. NOVAK

What are they going to do to you? Stand up to them!

VINCENT

There's two of them! They might beat me up; I don't know.

MRS. NOVAK

So that's why you stand at the window for a while after you leave the paper?

VINCENT

I'm waiting for them to find someone else to screw with. (Warily) How do you know I look out the window?

MRS. NOVAK

I see you through the eyehole; I peep. I don't get the paper 'til no one's here.

VINCENT

Don't you go anywhere? Out, I mean. What about groceries?

MRS. NOVAK

The doorman makes sure I get my deliveries. The landlord comes for his money just like you do.

VINCENT

Who do you talk to?

MRS. NOVAK

I'm talking to you, aren't I? You could be better than the radio. You come every day with the news, and you! You I can ask questions. We could talk while you're waiting for the Tylers to go away?

VINCENT

You want me to tell you the news?

MRS. NOVAK

(cautiously)

Especially the box scores. We'll call this our sanctuary, me and you. You wait, and we'll talk.

(FADE.)

(Lights up. VINCENT enters breathlessly from the service stairs door and walks to the doorway. MRS. NOVAK speaks before he can knock.)

MRS. NOVAK

Where've you been? I was beginning to think that you had forgotten about me today!

VINCENT

The Tylers were out in their front yard when I came down the block, so I sat down the behind a hedge and read the funnies until they went around back.

MRS. NOVAK

But now you're here! What has happened? What is the news?

VINCENT

The river caught fire!

MRS. NOVAK

The river? The Cuyahoga?

VINCENT

Yes, ma'am! It caught fire!

MRS. NOVAK

Why are you telling me this nonsense. Do you think I'm a fool?

VINCENT

Really! A couple of tugboats had to put it out.

MRS. NOVAK

How does water burn? Are you listening to the government? I think you are making fun of me.

VINCENT

I'm not making fun of you, Mrs. Novak. It's in the paper.

MRS. NOVAK

The front page will fool you, not the sports section. What about the Indians?

VINCENT

The Indians lost yesterday, 4 to 1.

MRS. NOVAK

Against the Orioles? That's not news.

VINCENT

Sims had a hit, but Williams gave up doubles to Buford and Frank Robinson.

MRS. NOVAK

We need to get some pitchers, we do. Why do you always tell me what Sims did? Is he your favorite player?

VINCENT

You bet. He catches, and he wears number eight. When he bats, you can tell that there's nothing that scares him. (pause) I wear number eight, too.

MRS. NOVAK

You play ball?

VINCENT

In the Tris Speaker League. I catch, too.

MRS. NOVAK

Is your team doing good? Are they winning?

VINCENT

Not bad. We're 6 and 6. My dad has coached every game we've won.

MRS. NOVAK

Coaching is your father's job?

VINCENT

He's the assistant. But our main coach doesn't show up half the time. One day he drove my dad and me to the game, and there were all these flat bottles rattling around under his seat.

MRS. NOVAK

So you must have fine baseball talk at the supper table each evening. I bet your mother is a good cook.

VINCENT

No. I only see him when he picks me up every week to go to the game. He and my mom are doing something called a trial separation.

MRS. NOVAK

Separation? What is that?

VINCENT

It's like try-outs for a divorce.

MRS. NOVAK

A divorce. That is America's plague, so sad. The one thing I give thanks for every day is how Mr. Novak loved me. (pause) I miss him so much.

VINCENT

I remember the day that the ambulance came. Do you ever go to the cemetery to visit? Leave some flowers?

MRS. NOVAK

I send Walter, the doorman. He tells me that the grave is very neat. What about your family? Do you have any brothers or sisters?

VINCENT

I have a little sister. She's in 4th grade. If I see the Tylers following us home, I'll tell her to run ahead while I stay back and distract them. She can't run very fast.

MRS. NOVAK

Is she a baseball fan too?

VINCENT

(Laughing) Yep, but her team is the Yankees. I don't know what's wrong with her. When there's a night game, you know, a late one after our bedtime, I used to sneak into my sister's room, and we'd sit by her window because it's over the driveway. My dad would be in the car down below with the windows open, listening to the game on the radio in his company car. We'd hear the announcer rise up through the cool night air and listen until we fell asleep. (Pause.) But now that he's not home, she cries sometimes after Mom tucks her in. Tucking in was Dad's job. I can hear her through the wall. So, when I hear her cry, I sneak outside her bedroom door, and I start pretending like I'm calling the Yankees game for the day. I read the box score, and I make up the action. I have Murcer and Pepitone hitting singles and doubles. I have Roy White making circus catches in leftfield, going over the wall.

(Lights shift and now VINCENT is sitting outside the door and his sister is on the other side of the door, crying softly in her bed.)

VINCENT

(Whispering through the door)

The Yankees are behind, 7–4, bottom of the ninth, and Joe Pepitone strides to the plate. Dave McNally shakes off the first two signs and then looks over his shoulder at Woods on second. The bases are loaded with Murcer on first and Horace Clarke on third. McNally winds up and throws a change up that has Pepitone swinging in the breeze. Strike one. McNally pitches from the stretch, and the next pitch is a curve ball that Pepitone watches fall in for strike two. Pepitone digs in with his back foot and watches McNally check Clarke at third. The crowd is on its feet and screaming for the Yanks. McNally stretches, and the pitch is a blazing fast ball, low and outside, and Pepitone reaches for it and clobbers the ball into deep center field. Blair turns and tracks the ball over his right shoulder. The Golden Glover sprints for the wall, hits the warning track, and then eases up as the ball sails over the wall. GRAND SLAM for Joe Pepitone. The Yanks win 8–7.

(Lights shift back to VINCENT in the hallway and MRS. NOVAK in the room.)

VINCENT (continued)

Even if the Yankees lose, I call it like they win, like they're heroes. I know she knows I'm making it up, but she never says anything, and she goes to sleep.

MRS. NOVAK

You're a good boy to look after her like that. Who looks after you?

VINCENT

My mom stays up late with the bills. She cries when she's washing the dishes sometimes. She can't afford to pick us up in the car, so that's why we walk home from school.

MRS. NOVAK

Sometimes you look out for yourself. (pause) You have to.

VINCENT

(Looking out the window to the yard below.)

It looks like the Tylers have chased after the ice cream truck. I'm going to finish my route now. Dad is supposed to come by to get some things this afternoon, and I don't want to miss him.

MRS. NOVAK

I hope your parents come to seeing the good. People should not wander from each other.

(FADE.)

(Lights up. VINCENT enters breathlessly from the service stairs door and walks to the doorway.)

VINCENT

They've done it! I saw pictures of them walking around!

MRS. NOVAK

What are you talking about? Who? Who's walking where?

VINCENT

Men! I've seen men walking on the moon!

MRS. NOVAK

Vincent! Why do you insist on telling me all this nonsense? I trust you to tell me the news.

VINCENT

Really! I saw it on TV. Neil Armstrong climbed out of the lunar thing and made footprints on the moon!

MRS. NOVAK

So far away! How could men do that?

VINCENT

It's the space race. President Kennedy said we could do it, said we could do it before the Russians.

MRS. NOVAK

The Russians, you say. What can the Russians do? I was born in Russia, and that is nearly as far away as the moon.

VINCENT

No, Mrs. Novak. They have planes that can take you there.

MRS. NOVAK

The Russia where I was born is farther than the moon. No one can go there anymore.

VINCENT

Sure. They have these big airliners that can go nonstop over the Atlantic Ocean. They serve you food and stuff.

MRS. NOVAK

The place where I was born is farther than the moon. When I was a girl, our village prospered. We took care of each other. Our families were the fabric that held the world together. Politics was just old men bickering over the chess tables in the park.

VINCENT

So it's all gone now? What happened to it?

MRS. NOVAK

The Bolsheviks came one November morning. Imagine a thousand Tylers, in long gray coats and black boots coming to break into your home. My mother was out in the street to face them. She carried a broom to beat them back. She told me to stay in the house, not to open the door to anybody. Never to open the door.

VINCENT

Where was your father? Did he try to protect you?

MRS. NOVAK

He was out there, too. The last thing he told me was not to open the door. I heard shots ring out. The crowd panicked and began running everywhere.

VINCENT

Did your mom and dad ever come home? Were they okay?

MRS. NOVAK

I never opened the door. I never saw them again.

VINCENT

But you were okay, right? You're here now.

MRS. NOVAK

Mr. Novak came to me from upstairs. He took me into his house, and he kept me safe.

VINCENT

And he kept you safe until last fall. But now you have nothing to be afraid of.

MRS. NOVAK

What do you know? What about the box scores? How did the Indians do in the last game of the series with the Tigers?

VINCENT

We lost. Suarez was catching, and Sims made an out pinch hitting. Kaline and Tresh pounded us.

MRS. NOVAK

It's been a trying year, no? Come close to the door. I have something for you.

(VINCENT stands directly in front of the door, and it opens very slightly so that MRS. NOVAK can slip her hand out through the crack and press a ticket into VINCENT'S hand. The door then immediately slams.)

MRS. NOVAK (continued)

Here. This is something I want you to have.

VINCENT

Mrs. Novak! This is a box seat for the Royals game!

MRS. NOVAK

I hope you like the game. The doorman can get me the tickets if I ask him. I told him to get a good seat.

VINCENT

This is the third base side right in front of the dugout, first row! This is super!

MRS. NOVAK

I wish I could have gotten a ticket for your father too. After you go, you come tell me about the game. I want a play-by-play.

VINCENT

Sure, Mrs. Novak, sure!
(FADE.)

(Lights up. VINCENT enters breathlessly from the service stairs door and runs to MRS. NOVAK'S door, beating frantically on it.)

Mrs. Novak! Mrs. Novak! The Tylers got in the door behind me! Let me in! Let me in! They're going to get me! Let me in!

(MRS. NOVAK runs to the door but does not open it. She peers through the peephole and sees the TYLER brothers run out of the delivery stairs and surround VINCENT. They rush VINCENT and begin beating him in the stomach. MRS. NOVAK watches through the peephole and sobs.)

MRS. NOVAK

Run! Run!

(The TYLER brothers pin VINCENT to the door and hit him repeatedly. VINCENT slumps to the ground, and the they drag him to the stairwell.)

MRS. NOVAK

Run, Papa, run!
(MRS. NOVAK slumps inside the door and sobs. FADE.)

(Lights up. VINCENT enters slowly from the service stairs door and places the paper on her threshold. He doesn't pause but immediately exits out the service stairs door. MRS. NOVAK watches silently from inside the door, watching through the peephole.)
(FADE.)

(Lights up. VINCENT enters slowly from the service stairs door and places the paper on her threshold. He pauses and takes a baseball from his pocket and lays it on top of the newspaper on the threshold.)

VINCENT

Duke Sims hit this ball. It was a ground ball foul, and I caught it when it bounced up into the box seats. I was right there on the front row. I brought it for you. (pause) When I got to the stadium and walked through the tunnel to the field on the second level, I never saw a field as green as the outfield. It was like a dream of grass. At first the players were small, like they are on TV, but when I got down to the first row, they were as big as life. I could hear them joking with each other. I could hear the ball popping into their mitts. The air was fresh off the lake, and I could smell tanned horsehide and tobacco spit.

MRS. NOVAK

Forgive me Vincent; please forgive me.

VINCENT

My mom gave me enough pocket money for a scorecard, and I kept track of all of the hits and runs, the outs and pitches, just like in the paper. I called the whole thing inside my head and wrote it down. But instead of having to make stuff up, there was more than I could take in. The crowd cheering and the smell of hot dogs and beer. The sun straight up and shining off the bases and the plate.

MRS. NOVAK

Please, Vincent. I just couldn't.

VINCENT

And the afternoon went on like I hoped it would never end. But we got off to a rough start when Fiore homered with two out, but at least Hargan made Foy look at strike three. Then they got three runs in the top of the third to lead at five to nothing. Duke Sims led off in the bottom of the third, but he struck out, and the next time he came up, they let Cap Petersen pinch hit for him. Duke rode out the rest of the game on the bench while the Royals racked up ten and shut us out.

MRS. NOVAK

There was nothing I could do.

VINCENT

After the game I stood by the dugout and yelled at Duke Sims to come sign my ball. At first he just grabbed his stuff and ignored everyone, but I kept hollering at him. Finally he came over to me and asked what the commotion was about. I told him that I'd caught his foul and asked him to sign it. He took the ball and looked around for a pen. A guy beside me shoved one in his hand. I told him I was sorry that they'd lost so bad, and that he'd gotten taken out so early. I told him that I wished they won every game. He looked at me and said, "How much fun would the game be if we won them all?" And then I thought about him standing at the plate, thousands of people screaming and his eyes completely fearless.

MRS. NOVAK

You are wise for your years, Vincent.

VINCENT

I'll see you tomorrow, Mrs. Novak.

The Poems

The Tehachapi Sheriff Buries His Native Wife Circa 1900

They saw me haul her out this morning
   Wrapped in canvas and the hides.
   Now they will not speak.
They saw me ride in alone at dusk
My horse slow and bearded with frost.

They know that having left her I slid down
   From wind-bitten light, followed the telegraph,
   Wire strung taut and cold as a nerve.
   They know this is the way to find Tehachapi
   When snow shakes down steep and stifle-deep.

Mr. Howard keeps the bar and hankers
   For the closing hour. Molly plays piano,
   Softly sings the refrain and sustains the final note.
   I sit alone.

They see December, thin smoke spin
   From stove-pipes, how the heart is skinned.
   They know I washed my wife with cold water,
   Clothed her in the gold-green gabardine.

The loungers drink deep, lick the suds
   From their long moustaches, hold their jokes.
   Boys circle and keep quiet.

They see me by the snapping stove, see
   How I abandoned my wife in hills and winter storm
   In the greatest room of her father.
   Do they see I could not wreck tools
   In the frozen church yard, laboring for a grave?
   Surely, no harm comes to the dead this way.

The card-players ring me, silent, watching. I pray
   For spring, when scent thickens, and buzzards
   Draw down and take eyes.

After Harvest

I t breaks within the sun-worn heads of men
   Who smell their death in cattle dung to hear
   The cock's mad crow at dusk as mocking them.

They stiffen in the dead part of their year.

It tightens in their raw-boned chests like dust
  Or silt, and tastes like the round, soured brows
  Of their good wives, their well's rich mossy rust.

It looks like their best friend, as each one knows.

And if they speak of it at all, they'll say
  It's just some sharpened pain that comes and goes,
  A finger lost to some blunt saw, a day
  They have forgotten, a worn-out pair of shoes.

But then tradition makes them form a ring,
  And drink. And like the silent earth, they sing.

Freeing the Sparrow

U ntil this moment
   He has never been
   Seen as clearly
As he is now.

His daughter watches
   From the green tangle
   Inside the garden
   As hand over hand
   Through the ripped
   Tomato netting
   He works toward
   The sparrow's wary eye.

The small round world
   Holds steady
   Despite the beating
   Of the tangled wings;
   His daughter
   Holds the moment
   Under her breath.

He struggles
   To hold this

Moment, too small
Almost to fit
In his hand;
He unwinds, carefully,
Braided green cotton
From dun feather,
Knotted mesh frayed
From tiny hollow talon,
The world's tangle
From his child's hope.

At last!
Raised gently skyward,
The sparrow's quick wings
Mix up the air;
The moment fixed,
His daughter turns
Back toward the world;

The father turns
Also, untangled
From his daughter's stare.

Pride and Joy

Late afternoon, early spring,
When dogwoods bloom outside the window,
I try to steal some time
For myself, cradle the banjo,
And my hand hovers the strings.
I'm trying to steal an older time, too,

As I finger the first phrase
Of "Soldier's Joy;" the melody dips
Down to low D, slips back up the scale
By thirds, and the notes throb and pop
Off the head's tense skin.
Time slides backward; I recall

My grandmother's trembling chin,
Her voice rise over the kitchen sink, carry
Out the window screen into the evening
Deepening toward fall:
"I'm my momma's pride and joy…"
I ran from the house to play

In the last light, past where the paperboy
Threw the morning news, forgotten
In the tall grass, the headline lying

Face down and crying,
"Boys Are Coming Home."
Everywhere the horizon darkens,

And my right hand wrings my inheritance
From the banjo's wood and brass.
I treasure the tune like a letter from home and long
For more, homesick as any inmate,
Gazing at the dogwoods and the past
Through the bars of a song.

The Last Thing You Wanted

The last name of your second grade teacher,
    the last costume you wore for Halloween,
    the last morning you kissed your grandmother,
the last place you knew you shouldn't have been,
the last three digits of your license plate,
the last amount of the electric bill,
the last increase of the postage rate,
the last evening you heard a whippoorwill,
the last drawer where you hunted your keys,
the last appointment that went unmet,
the last stoplight where you knew your way,
the last meal you knew where everyone sat,
the first time you noticed my face and how,
despite its concern, it was nameless now.

Ice Storm

All evening we listened to the sky
      fall into the trees.
      As the dusk gathered, grain by grain,
the weight accumulated
until the great branches creaked.
Around the house the old boughs bowed, touched their knuckles
to our windowpanes.

Then, at the yard's edge, one branch buckled.
   Soon a limb knocked the mailbox from its post.
   And as the darkness fell, far off and close,
   We found the sounds of each tree's ruin
   betrayed its species:
   at the breaking point, pines popped
   like potshots, plummeted from treetops;
   but the oaks surrendered when one sinew split,
   and the limb, shoulder-ripped, tipped earthward,
   arcing through the hundred years
   It had risen in the air,
   crashed like a chandelier;
   crystals skittered across the porch.

After midnight, as we heard the silent storm
   wreck the architecture of the woods,

came what we expected:
the nightlight extinguished, the subterranean thrum
Of the furnace ceased.
The cedar lay down on the cellar door.
When in the room's stillness we could smell the cold,
we called the kids into our bed.
From the top of the linen closet, the quilts
came down, and we settled under their weight.
We heard the ice mantle and dismantle the forest,
holding one another for heat.

Toward dawn, nodding in our wooden shell
  we did not know
  what world light would reveal.
  We knew we could not know
  of those we held, in that blanketed embrace,
  parent and child,
  companion and spouse,
  who might fall,
  who would bear up.

Insurance Trilogy

I. Appraiser

Late afternoon I visit the body
    Shop, east L.A. and hard sun
Shattered in the cluttered yard.

Mechanics gape from bays as I fiddle
    With forms, loss
    Sheets, ask which car it is.

The garage owner threads me back
    To the total, looks sideways, through his teeth
    Says this one ain't so bad.

He's shown me the Polaroids he has
    Tacked up in the welding shed.
    One shows a boy's face laying in a bucket seat.

He stares at this one first thing
    Each morning, wonders
    How it got there.

This wreck is just a head–
    On. I detail

What steel has done

To steel, the rending and wild stress,
   Like what a mean question can do
   To a person.

I take down numbers, evaluate
   The paint, the windshield cracked like a web
   From a bulge on the driver's side.

In the center hangs a blonde hair-hank.
   I yank the door and breathe
   Hot vinyl and perfume.

Even this far in-
   Land the wind is raw with salt.
   I lay down my clipboard and think fast

Cars and bare beaches. I slide my hands
   Out of my pockets and comb my hair.
   I envision girls asleep

At the wheel.

I get back
   To business. I write
   Down the license tag. I hunt

For salvage.
   I stand back and reckon the damage.
   I take out my camera, take pictures.

II. Adjustor

The way the sun leans down on Watts
  Is how a man can lean for years
  Against an orange crate in a vacant lot.

I'm bickering over twenty stitches a bottle
  Ripped in the Korean grocer's ear.
  He complains the way the sun leans down on Watts

Out the screen door on the dude who's shot
  Around the eyes, like me, from wanting a woman and a beer.
  We slip out needy hands, draw vacant lots.

Everyone here dreams the same dream and its rotten.
  If you cored the family Bible and the high school years
  You'd find the pit bitten by the sun that leans on Watts.

My dreams drag me like harried cops
  To take statements from old black women sheared
  Of their purses, squalling hard in vacant lots.

After supper I'll miss the deliberate way she washed the dishes. I'll clear
  The rickety table under the kitchen bulb. The light is near
  The way the sun leans down on Watts
  Against an orange crate in a vacant lot.

III. Restitution

I know what a leg is worth.

I know what is and isn't the full use of a hand.

I can calculate pain and suffering,
    Which man hurts and which man's bluffing.

I'll pay a pretty girl extra for a scar.

I drive like Jesus in a company car
    All over L.A. restoring the broken with company money.

I have sheets where I can figure
    The years of wages a man has lost
    Because some Monday morning he misunderstood

The foreman, thought he said, let it go
    Instead of, take it slow, and his hard-hat squirted
    From under the concrete wall.

I'll hand the widow the check for the wrong-
    Ful death, money that will run
    Out too fast in Bakersfield or Fresno.

She holds the thousands of dollars the way she might
    Have held his calloused hand on a June night after supper
    When the sun set late in savings time
    And everything was right.

Voyeur

Envision, this evening
    as June pulses in the green veins
    of every vine,
this very magnolia blossom
revolving in the bowl
on the vacant countertop.

Fresh-cut, it vaguely opened,
    its vivid pistils waving
    in a pallid vulva;
    it unveiled its fragrance
    invisibly, its vapors
    vitally everywhere.

But now, inevitably,
    after a week's visit,
    the leaves are a lovely
    tea-stained vellum,
    a rusted velvet.
    Move along now;

this poem's over.

Under Our Daughter's Bed

After her wedding, her mother and I
  While boxing up some things for her new home
  Comb through the history beneath her bed
Like archeologists working backward
Through all the dregs and treasures of her youth:
Some Cosmopolitans and scratched CD's,
A wadded pack of cigarettes, a knife,
The crumpled break-up letter from an ex,
The teddy bear she hugged between her thighs
Her last night as a girl, a plastic bag
Of baby teeth, part of the purse she clutched
First day of school, a doll's lost rolling eye,
A tattered costume veil she used to wear—
Remember? She said she would marry me.

The Onion Cutters

Families depend on them, alone
    In the kitchen, loved ones
    Willing to weep for their suppers,

Like the sister who slices the paper skin.
  As the kitchen fills with sudden tears,
  She feels the dull-edged knife
  Press the bulb of her thumb
  And envies the kin who all have wives.

Or the grandfather who whistles, and wears
  His wedding band, still,
  Wielding the blade under cold running water,
  The onion revolving in his hands turning numb.
  His wife's been buried for twenty years.

Or the mother who halves the layered globe
  After she brings her daughter home
  From the abortionist's office, tucks her in
  Upstairs, clicks off the cartoons, gently closes
  The door of the closet where the monsters
  Hold each other.

Whippoorwill

In that crepuscular hour
    when the crisp edge
    of the oak leaf blurs
and fades in the failing light
until it is inextricable
from the backing sky,
the night is jarred
by the whippoorwill
repeating its name
in incessant narcissism.

I have never seen
    its cryptic plumage
    or nestless dwelling place
    in the litter of the undergrowth.
    I may have stepped an egg's width
    from its white-tipped tail,
    but it has never flown.
    It cartwheels over the grass-tips
    of the invisible meadow
    and feeds at the whim of the moon.

Because I have never seen
    the whiskered beak,

the bark-like feathers
clumped as it sleeps
on a locust limb, unruffled
by the dappled noon
playing on its back
or the rain flicking
through the flinching leaves,
the whippoorwill has tricked me

into speaking its language.

Now, from the wood's edge
    its cretic call fills the night, resonates everywhere.
    The note is wistful as a child's whistle
    at deepest dusk. A recollection
    of coming home, long past supper,
    unseen on the sidewalk
    beyond the rectangle of light

thrown from the kitchen window,
    like the whippoorwill,

has named itself.

Sandy Hook

How can we tell
our children
our children
can be taken
by the chaos
of the world?

How many times
will we wake
in night's cradle
to listen to wind
swallow the world?

Eros Peractorum

She wants him, though she spoiled the chance
to wed when they were younger.
She clings to her remembrances,
the boy he is no longer.
And what she wants and recollects
are like a song filled with regret;
the words and music both reflect
nostalgia growing stronger.

She had to choose between two men
Just to escape her father.
Her prudence made her pick the one
who'd prize but never love her.
Now every afternoon is grayed
with decisions she should have made;
She wishes that she would have stayed
True to her first true lover.

Her memory is like a room
he carries deep inside him.
To him, her voice is like a tune
that echoes deep inside it.
But all the miles and all the days
have dimmed the melody's refrain;

her voice is softer now than rain
that whispers far behind him.

The empty room exacerbates
her loneliness and sorrow;
the silence that floods through her days
makes her regret tomorrow.
Her memory becomes a place
where she can hide and she can trace
the last sound of her happiness,
a cold and silent sparrow.

Then one day she can stand no more
and finds the strength to call him.
He's startled by her voice, implored
to pick up what has fallen.
And though he understands her plea
and treasures how they used to be
he strains to gently make her see
that time has just undone them.

And in the silence that ensues
they listen for each other.
Each breathless, stark heartbeat subdues
their history as lovers.
Her life is like a wistful tune
and his a strange and foreign room;
the silence in between them proves
that they have lost each other.

History

Home from summer
     classes at college,
     my daughter topples
her stack of books
on the tabletop—
Physics, finite math,
American History
from 1860.
Listlessly, she thumbs
the texts, stops
on the chapter
about Viet Nam
and asks me
to quiz her.

We review the French
    withdrawal, American
    advisors, the reasons
    Lyndon Johnson built
    up the troops, and names
    like Dien Bien Phu,
    Operation Arc Light,
    Westmoreland and Ho
    Chi Minh, the ARVN

and Tet, Khe Sahn.
The fall of Saigon.

Outside the window,
   the summer sun
   stuns the afternoon
   with relentless light,
   and my daughter
   nods in the central air,
   slides a blue plate
   of tomatoes
   toward me, surrenders
   her head to the comfort
   of her folded arms
   on the tablecloth.

I should tell her

about the tomatoes
   at her elbow,
   how the salted slices
   were my grandmother's favorite—
   how I wrapped the plate
   in embroidered dish towels
   the afternoon
   we returned
   from her funeral—
   how warm Early Girls
   sat on her tongue
   in late July
   the hour before the telegram
   arrived, and how
   her supper congealed

on that blue plate
as I watched, in the other
room, the impossible journey
of men returning

from the moon.

Equinox

Spring shows up, familiar as the mail truck
    On this Tuesday morning, rain peppering
    The sidewalk, the smell of earthworms blooming
At the bus stop, one shoe hopelessly stuck
In a galosh, the clouds so thick the lights
Stay on 'til noon, and her face reflected
In the dark window. This humid lesson
Suggests balance: right and wrong, day and night.

So I relish the ride home, finding her
    Beneath the awning in her yellow coat,
    Raising her into the rain-slicked basket
Of my slippery bicycle, our ears
Filling with rain as we pedal and coast
Through the curtains of our newest banquet.

Pep Squad, 1967

The most thumb-worn photo in my album
  Pictures my wife in her cheer-leading uniform,
  Nine years old, a beehive hairdo,
Waving: an oblivious time-traveler.

Tonight her profile at bedtime
  Reminds me of that earnest pose
  And her serious smile for the camera,
  A girl I'll never meet.

Unbelievable, really, but here
  She is, and my photo app
  Strives to frame how I love her
  As she grins from the kitchen sink.

Photos are glimpsed windows,
  And inside them, people are captured
  In their happiness or something
  We have to guess. Yes,

I realize we'll all be
  Captives, faded but young, shuttered,
  Smiling and waving at those
  Who live outside our time.

Viral Spring

Worlds ago, my college French professor,
a debutante's grandmother in support hose
who gently tried to tune our southern accents
to the delicate music of words like "oeil"
and "mer," promised me
that one day I would know I had mastered that tongue
when I spoke it in my dreams.
In the last semester of my senior year,
I woke remembering a black-haired girl had just asked me
for the time, "quelle heure est-il," and I had replied
"Je ne sais pas," I don't know.

This morning I wake from recursive scraps of nightmare,
empty eyes above a blue mask, a wet-faced girl who won't keep
six feet away, hospital clocks with their hands on their faces,
my mother reaching for me from the other side
of the wire-reinforced glass.
In just weeks I am fluent in this isolated country
where we are besieged by nothing
we can see, apprehensive of everything.
"Community spread," "Social distancing," "flattening the curve," "N95."
Like years ago, I mouth them into memory.
Quelle heure et-il? Je ne sais pas.

The Last Tattoo Poem

Forty years ago
   I began
      To fill my arms with beasts.

I saved my pay
   For Charlie, the Hell's Angel,
   On the corner of Victory

And Van Nuys, his needle
   Driving my dreams
   Underneath my skin,

The eagle, tiger,
   Peacock and rose, the dragon
   Breathing fire,

The reaper staring down
   All of my days.
   Charlie scribed the armor

I wore in the rumbling saddle
   Of my Harley iron
   In the valley of L.A.

***

But time gnaws
   Everything, flesh and steel.
   The days have dulled

The eagle's sharpened eye,
   The peacock's talon,
   The tiger's fang and claw,

The rose's thorn.
   The dragon's flame has withered.
   I have burned

Through a thousand skins.
   Millions of minutes
   Have worn me thin; I've been

Weathered by love
   And death and countless afternoons
   When nothing happened.

***

What persists is the core
   Of the self-inflicted scar.
   The reason why

I volunteered for pain.
   Every stare
   Confirms these marks

Are more than skin
    Deep. Take, for instance,
    The scripture scripted

Over my heart,
    Chapter and verse,
    The gospel faded

Back into tongues.

Christmas, the Psychiatric Hospital, the Magi

Bidden by some strange god who whirls
  In the darkness of our anxious heads,
  We have come to find
Lab men can only tell us
It has something to do with seratonin,
High-line wires snapping in brain-storm.

Last night no star. Flare
  And sizzle of power shorting out
  On crosspoles north of a town
  Where the wind blows so relentlessly
  We are sure nobody loves us.

Medic, goddamn it, bring us
  Relief. Lithium's gift is empty
  As myrrh and frankincense.
  Show us the miracle
  That will bring our thoughts back
  To the right part of our brains.

Seven a.m. makes us think
  No tomorrow. The poinsettia leaf

Sharpens on the coffee table.
We feel our bones and fear them.

Chosen, we have brought our terrible wisdom
   To witness the birth
   Of peace in our wide-eyed heads.
   We have come through
   Menacingly still fields, rooms
   Where our parents ranted under chandeliers,
   Doors still hanging open where lovers left.

Divorce and panic, at least one
   Of us has tried to thieve
   His own life. Teach us
   New prayers for the hometowns
   That have died in our absence.

Give us each strength to climb back,
   leg-heavy, to our own country,
   To face our people,

Tell them what we know.

Fossil

Studiously stooped, fists on thighs,
   my grandson eyeballs a rock
   working out of the clay

of our rutted driveway,
   straightens slowly up, sighs,
   and kicks it free;

he's almost three,
   generous in his ways,
   so raises the gift to me,

a chunk of limestone, worn
   and clay-stained, veined with age,
   ocean-stone air-borne

in my freckled right hand,
   a shard of sea-floor
   unlocked from land, and, behold—

a brachiopod! Well, no—
   its imprint, a delicate fan
   the size of a moth's wing,

an engraving of fragile ribs
    from millennia before
    the dinosaurs.

When we leave
    what do we leave
    behind?

Not so bad, to slip into the flow
    of years, years from now
    when he is a grandfather

and I am gone.
    I believe he will feel
    my impression

when he picks up
    and holds
    my banjo, my watch, my hammer.